His arrogance fired Jenni's anger.

"You're so used to women agreeing with you you can't understand when they don't." Jenni was really warming to her theme.

"But I'm not one of them. I'm not in the least in awe of you—or your money. As a man you mean nothing to me."

They stared at each other, and she saw the blaze of anger in his eyes. It was a long time before he spoke, and to her surprise his tones were calm and even. "Do you really think," he said, an edge of laughter in his voice, "that I couldn't have you eating out of my hand? If I were to do that—" he snapped his fingers "—you would react the same as every other woman I've met."

Catch a Star

Alexandra Scott

Harlequin Books

TORONTO • NEW YORK • LOS ANGELES • LONDON
AMSTERDAM • PARIS • SYDNEY • HAMBURG
STOCKHOLM • ATHENS • TOKYO • MILAN

Original hardcover edition published in 1982
by Mills & Boon Limited

ISBN 0-373-02554-8

Harlequin Romance first edition June 1983

CHAPTER ONE

'You wouldn't be here at all if I could have prevented it. You realise that I suppose, Miss Cotterell?'

Jenni stared angrily back across the vast expanse of desk at the dark-visaged stranger, trying to equate him with the man she had heard so much chatter about last month. Then, becoming aware of the coldness of his appraising expression, she felt the slow colour rise in her cheeks. 'Yes, you've made your feelings abundantly clear, Mr Drimakos. I can see that my presence is unwelcome to you, only . . .'

'Only . . .' his interruption was as arrogant as the rest of him with little regard for the normal social niceties, 'I hope you aren't going to tell me how sorry you are for your sister, for quite frankly, Miss Cotterell, I'm not interested. I'm tired of all the troubles caused by this marriage, tired of the constant disruption *my* sister has had to endure, and having to cope with your precipitate arrival is just about the last straw. It's time your sister came to her senses and . . .'

'And your nephew.' Coolly calculating, Jenni interrupted with the same sarcasm he had shown. The intense blue eyes, normally so tolerant, flashed with sudden rage which she took no trouble to conceal. 'In these situations I find that the faults are rarely on one side.'

'That is true.' His words were still more clipped, so she realised she had irritated him even more. 'Giannis has many faults, the major one being that he has been too tolerant. Long ago he should have shown his wife

5

who was master, then there would have been no question of her running away to South America.'

Between them smouldered a question that Jenni longed to ask, one that she sensed would have given him great satisfaction to answer, thus one that had to be postponed. Instead she made the only comment she could think of that was disparaging.

'I'm afraid young women are no longer like that, Mr Drimakos.' The slightly mocking tone was calculated to annoy most men, especially one like Perikles Drimakos, and as she saw his lips tighten, a tiny shiver of satisfaction ran down her spine. 'They're no longer willing to be told what to do, where to go, to be at the beck and call of a man, husband or not, and . . .'

'You must not assume such an air of authority about matters of which you are ignorant, Miss Cotterell.' As he spoke he rose from his chair, looking down at her from the opposite side of his desk, the curious eyes narrowed faintly. 'All women prefer a man to be master in his own house, that is a rule with no exceptions. It is a subject I know a great deal about—believe me!' For a moment the shadow of a smile flickered about the thinnish lips, but it was so quickly gone that Jenni was left wondering if she had imagined that flicker of humour. Her mind returned to what he had just said.

A subject he knew a great deal about. Apprehension quivered through her. She did believe him, easily. The tall powerful man facing her would dominate not only the women in his life but most men too, she decided. She searched around in the back of her mind for what she knew about him, discovering to her surprise that there was very little, in spite of Dina's chatter. There had been no mention of a wife, she recalled, although it was more than likely that a man in his mid-thirties would be married.

Studying him, she decided that he was taller than the average Greek. Even with her brief experiences—she had arrived in Athens exactly two hours earlier—she knew that Greek men were on the short side. And in other ways too he differed from her idea of the typical Greek, although he was dark like most Mediterranean races. He had high cheekbones and long tilted eyes, black and shining with a hint of Tartar blood but unexpectedly attractive in spite of the cold penetrating way he looked at her. His hair was almost jet black, gleaming like his eyes, long and immaculately cut so that it clung, waving only slightly, to his head.

'However, Miss Cotterell,' his interruption of her scrutiny brought her gaze back to those knowing sardonic eyes, 'you are here now and I have no choice but to accept it. So if you care to come with me I shall take you to my sister's house. The child is there, as I told you.' He walked round the desk waiting while she reached for the large brown grip which held her travel documents, paperbacks and things she had wanted during the flight.

When she stood up and faced him she noticed again that look of faint surprise which had been so apparent when she had first been shown into his office, and his next words, spoken for the first time in a normal conversational tone, confirmed that look. 'So *you* are Angela's sister!' It was a statement, but the question was implicit, and understanding the cause she coloured angrily.

'Stepsister, actually.' She forced a drawl into her well-modulated voice. 'There's no blood relationship.' She paused while they walked together across the pale marble floor, smiling up at him as she walked through the door he held open for her. 'And you are Giannis's uncle.' It was an echo of his own incredulity and just

as much deserved. For while her own appearance was
as far from Angie's petite prettiness as it was possible
to be, equally Giannis with his slight build and gentle
manners had nothing of his uncle in him.

Apparently her comment deserved no reply, for he
was silent as they walked through the outer office
where his secretary was still busily working away at
her typewriter and silent as they travelled down in the
lift, sliding rapidly from the top floor where his palatial
offices were located. Just for a few moments Jenni had
the opportunity to study her reflection in the tinted
glass of the large brass-framed mirror on the wall of
the elevator, and with a sickening little jolt of her
spirits she understood why he had doubted her relationship with Angela.

Even at her best she could scarcely compete, and the
long tiring trip had done nothing for her appearance.
It was just a pity that she had her hair pulled back in a
ponytail, secured by an elastic band. Since she had
grown it long it had developed a tendency to curl and
this was the most obvious way of keeping it under control, especially in class. And the dress she was wearing
did nothing for her, even if Jeremy had chosen it for
her. These long flowing ethnic lines were out and the
colour, a dull russety shade, was too much like her
hair, and made her seem faded. A spasm of dissatisfac-
tion swept through her as the image of Angela danced
before her eyes.

'This way.' He didn't even pause to wait for her,
simply walked from the lift towards the huge plate glass
doors which excluded the overwhelming heat of the
afternoon from the cool air-conditioned interior,
nodding briefly to the uniformed man who stepped
forward to hold the door.

At a signal from the doorman the long white car

which had collected Jenni from the airport slid to a halt in front of them and Jenni found herself ushered into the back while her escort gave rapid instructions to the chauffeur. A moment later they were nosing out into the mainstream of the traffic and Jenni sat back, determined in spite of everything to enjoy the unusual luxury of the strange situation.

Two nights ago that frantic telephone call from her stepsister had taken her entirely by surprise, for she had only just returned to normal after the traumatic experience of sharing her small Croydon flat with Angela and Dina. Pleased as she had been to see them at first, the cramped conditions had soon rubbed the gilt from the gingerbread, and it was hard as well to avoid the conviction that the child was thoroughly spoiled and used to having her own way in everything.

Although Jenni had pressed her, Angela had refused to admit that there was anything wrong with her marriage, had pretended that the only reason for her prolonged visit to England was a simple case of homesickness. But how she could feel homesick when she and Giannis had spent the six years since their marriage traipsing round the world with frequent stops in London, Jenni couldn't understand. It wasn't as if she had ever shown any sign of missing England and family until this unexpected visit.

And then there was the fact that almost every night she had gone out, leaving Jenni to babysit with the five-year-old Dina.

'You're sure you don't mind, Jenni darling?' Since she had married Giannis, Angela had developed an entrancing accent which reminded everyone she met of Nana Mouskouri. Jenni was the only one who suspected that was as far as her Greek extended, for she seemed unable to understand even her daughter's simple conversation unless the little girl could be persuaded to speak English. 'It's so rude, darling,' Angie would pout at her, 'when Jenni doesn't speak Greek.'

And the child would give her one of those droll knowing looks, then perhaps would allow herself to be cajoled or bribed into agreeing. Just as Jenni always agreed to babysit.

'Of course I don't mind.' But something inside her was anxious as she watched the care with which her stepsister applied her make-up, noticed the bright excited gleam in her eyes. 'If only I knew where you were going Angie. What if I should have to get in touch with you, what if Dina became ill, what if Giannis should call?'

'Then he can call again. And as to Dina, that child's as tough as old boots.'

'Angela!'

'It's true.' Angela smiled her perfect, selfish smile as she turned from the mirror. 'She's never had a day's illness in her life. Besides, she loves being with you. I don't know anyone else she likes half as much. It's a good thing I'm not a jealous kind of mother.'

But it doesn't suit you to be that right at this moment, thought Jenni, then instantly dismissed the idea as ungenerous. And there was something in what Angela said; Dina was slightly more amenable with her than she was with her mother.

'What time is Jeremy coming round?' Usually Angela had remembered to ask.

'Oh, about eight, he said.'

'That's all right, then. Be good!' And with that last admonition Angela would dash off in a haze of exotic scent and looking totally out of place in Ellis Court.

Be good. Once or twice Jenni reflected on that advice with a wry smile as she began to make the meal for herself and Jeremy. Life with Angela always seemed to be the wrong way round. It had always been like that. Ever since the four-year-old and the seven-year-old had become stepsisters almost twenty years earlier! Jenni had been the one who was protective while Angie was bold and daring, always in hot water but somehow always emerging from it unscathed. And usually with a quip, a word of advice for her duller older sister. Even when their parents had died, first Angela's father, then Jenni's mother, Jenni was the one who cared for things, Angela had laughed at life.

'Be good? With Jeremy? Her cheeks coloured at the implication of the remark while her hands were busy with the vegetables she was chopping for the curry they were going to eat that evening. She wasn't totally familiar with vegetarian diet as yet and she couldn't get the meal ready within thinking as she would have have been able to do with an ordinary meat dish. She had to concentrate otherwise she might make a mistake and use some animal fat which Jeremy would be sure to detect. That had happened the other night, and it was the first time she had seen him annoyed. Not that he had said a lot, but she had known. He was so intense about things, took everything so seriously.

And of course he was right. It was true what he said—all of it. At least most of it. She *did* agree with most of it. Some of his more extreme ideas she could see wouldn't work out. Even if they ever saved enough to buy a Welsh hill farm she didn't know that it would be so easy to become completely self-supporting, but she sympathised with the idea. And it was nice for him to have his dreams—which was all they would ever be. There wasn't much chance of him putting enough aside from his salary as a social worker and the heavy expenses of living in Croydon didn't leave a great deal from her teaching salary. No, it would remain a dream. Poor darling! But in the meantime she was prepared to go along with him—natural foods, a return to a simpler way of life. It was something to think about even if in their totally urban setting it was impossible to pursue. She had the feeling that when they married they would be just like most of their colleagues, content to settle for a small semi, with a patch of garden and a mortgage that they might have to hand on to their children. But there was one thing she was certain of, with Jeremy she would be *good*, as Angela put it. For he had principles.

'As I told you, Miss Cotterell,' Perikles Drimakos brought her back to the present again, 'I think it would be best if you were to take Dina back to her parents' home, at least for the time being.' He was leaning back in the corner of the rear seat, one arm extended along the back. There was something about him that drew Jenni's eyes against her inclination, something that made her notice again the breadth of the shoulders in the fine brown jacket, the suggestion of dark hair beneath the cream silk shirt. As she looked at him one hand came up to cover his mouth and the long forefinger stroked the dark cheek. She heard the faint rasp of a beard and withdrew her eyes, looking with a sense of desperation through the tinted glass out into the teeming crowded streets, unable to understand her own emotions.

'Very well.' Her voice seemed to be coming from a distance and she had lost any inclination to fence with him.

'Yes. My sister isn't strong and the child's behaviour has been outrageous. Merope isn't fit to be troubled and must have a rest. Besides, Dina might be happier in her own home with all her toys about her. Although,' now he appeared to be speaking almost to himself, regretfully, 'they spend little enough time there in fact.'

There was a long silence while Jenni tried feverishly, unsuccessfully to think of something to say, and before she could do so it was her companion who spoke again, this time with the polite expressions of interest which might have been looked for earlier.

'You have no reason to hurry back to London, Miss Cotterell?'

'I should have.' It was a comfort to let him know at last that his family wasn't the only one to be put to considerable inconvenience. 'I had to make some frantic arrangements when I got the telephone call. It was only because Angie sounded so distraught that I did. As it was, my employers,' she turned to find him still looking in her direction, 'were by no means pleased. You know I teach English and history in a private school. I'm not even certain that they'll be willing to have me back. It isn't fair on them to leave at such short notice.'

'Well, surely in an emergency they must make allowances.'

Jenni shrugged, glad to have the chance of making the most of her sacrifice. 'Well, I don't know. It might even affect my pension if I can't get a job when I go back.'

'How old are you, Miss Cotterell?' Something in his voice made her look at him with suspicion but there was no suggestion of amusement on his face.

'I'm twenty-six.' Nearly twenty-seven, she reminded herself with a shade of anxiety, but still she felt idiotic about that remark concerning her pension. What had made her say that to him, a man who could pay all the pensions in Croydon and never miss the money? And it wasn't what she had meant to say. It was just that

Jeremy was always emphasising the value of a state pension, working out just how well off they'd be in Wales at some distant time in the future, when he was sixty-five and she was just sixty. There were times when he was just a bit inclined to live in the future and to forget about the present.

Just then Jenni realised that they had turned out of the busy stream of traffic into a quiet road of residential villas, most of them shielded from curious eyes by high hedges of flowering shrubs, the entrances guarded by solid wooden or metal gates. It was at one of these that they stopped and Jenni watched while the chauffeur got out of the car, stood for a moment in front of one of the stone pillars with a sort of grille set into it before coming back to the car.

Almost immediately the gate swung open of its own accord and the car was able to proceed along the drive which curved upwards from the road. Jenni was unable to resist a backward glance and saw the gates close with a faint clanging sound. Aware of a pair of eyes on her, she looked at her companion and raised an enquiring eyebrow.

'Yes, the Athenians are very security-conscious, I'm afraid.' His expression was more relaxed than it had been since they met and the broad shoulders rippled the well fitting jacket with a shrug. 'I suppose it's that we've always lived under threat of attack. There's nothing like it for concentrating the mind. Well, here we are.' The car slid to a halt in front of the huge villa and his attention was at once transferred from Jenni's face to the large windows looking blankly down at them.

A moment later they were mounting the few steps to the heavy oak front door and Jenni was very conscious of the hand on her elbow as for the first time Perikles

Drimakos treated her like a woman. But before she had time to do more than notice it the door was thrown open with some violence, a voice in rapid Greek spoke in remonstrance, made a shushing sound, and then a small figure literally threw herself at Jenni with such force that she would have unbalanced without that stabilising touch.

'Auntie Jen! Auntie Jen!' Dina sobbed as she wrapped her arms about Jenni's neck, and as the girl straightened up she noticed the way Perikles Drimakos's narrow lips tightened before he at once turned to the figure hovering just inside the open doorway and addressed her in rapid enquiry.

'Hush, baby, hush!' Carrying the child uncomfortably because of the legs wrapped tightly about her waist, the arms suffocatingly round her neck, Jenni spoke as soothingly as she could into the cloud of dark hair. But her eyes were following the man, watching while he frowned over the reply he got from the elderly woman who was so obviously a servant and who as she spoke at voluble length shook her head repeatedly while she looked reprovingly at the child.

'Come on now, darling.' Jenni tried to disentangle herself from the throttling embrace as she stepped over the threshold of the house. 'It isn't as bad as that.'

'It is! It is!' Dina raised a tear-stained face. 'It is bad. I want to go ho—ome!'

'Be quiet, Dina!' Her uncle's voice was cold and intolerant. 'You are going home. That's exactly why Miss Cotterell has come.'

'Miss Cottle?' Dina turned to look at the disapproving faces of her uncle and the servant.

'Jenni. Your Aunt Jenni has come to take you home.'

Dina stared at him, stopping sobbing for the first

time since their arrival and putting up an arm to brush some of the tears from her swollen face. Then she turned to Jenni, her lower lip trembling. 'You're taking me home, Auntie Jen?'

'Yes.' Feeling curiously close to tears herself, Jenni tried to smile. 'But only if you're very good, darling.'

'In the meantime,' her uncle interrupted brusquely, 'you will go with Magda while I take your aunt to visit your grandmother. Do you understand?'

The small figure, still supported in Jenni's arms, twisted round so that she was looking into the intimidating face of the man. 'I don't like you now, Uncle Peri.' Powerful sincerity sounded in her childish tones and Jenni held her breath, relaxing only when he turned away.

'Magda is my sister's companion, Miss Cotterell.' He spoke over his shoulder while he stopped by a table to pick up some papers. 'Magda, this is Miss Cotterell, Angela's sister.'

The old woman smiled faintly, but once again Jenni sensed a slight scepticism as the woman's dark eyes noticed her features before moving on to her dress.

'Now go with Magda as I told you, Dina.' His tone was only a little less harsh now, but Jenni was relieved to feel a slackening of the child's arms as she allowed her to slip to the floor.

'Are you really taking me home, Auntie Jen?' Dina still retained hold of one of Jenni's hands while she put her question.

'Yes, just for a little while, darling.' Jenni was uncertain what she was committing herself to and her reply was wary. 'Just till your mummy comes back.'

'My mummy isn't coming back.'

'Of course . . .' Jenni straightened up, realising just how little she knew about the situation. 'Anyway, we'll talk about it later. Now go with Magda and be a good girl.'

When the child and the woman had gone through a door behind the wide curving staircase Jenni had time at last to notice her surroundings, to realise just how sumptuous they were. The hall was shadowy with windows shuttered against the heat of the sun and cooled by the pale green of the marble floor. Here and there in alcoves about the walls were pieces of sculpture and ceramic ware and at the foot of the staircase in a huge terracotta container was a mass of fernlike plants.

'If you would come this way, Miss Cotterell.' Perikles Drimakos began to mount the stairs and still looking about her Jenni followed, her flat shoes making flopping sounds on the marble treads. 'What do you think of the house?' He cast a keen sideways glance in her direction.

'It's beautiful, of course. I've never seen one like it, but . . .' That last tiny betraying word escaped before she could stop it, and as she might have expected he seized on it at once.

'But . . .?' He sounded as if it were a challenge.

'But . . .' She thought quickly, unwilling to say what she thought that it was scarcely homelike. '. . . I should be afraid to touch any of the beautiful ornaments in case I should damage any of them. They must be priceless.'

'Oh, is that all? I had the idea you were going to say something else.'

When they reached the upper landing Jenni could see that the circular landing was richly carpeted in pale green and had a series of doors, all firmly closed set round the walls.

Still looking at her with that sardonic irritating expression, he walked forward to one of them and knocked, then opened it and went inside, gesturing to Jenni that she should follow. Before she had time to notice the occupant Jenni's eyes were drawn to the glorious panorama visible through floor-length windows thrown open on to a small balcony, a view that seemed to encompass the heavenly incredible blue of sky and sea, some distant hazy humps of islands and a scattering of sails with here and there the darker outlines, the trailing smoke of steamers.

But before she had time to comment she was being taken over to a sofa pulled up close to the window. She watched while Perikles Drimakos bent down to kiss the woman who was lying there, saw how his hand lingered affectionately against her cheek. She didn't understand the words that were exchanged but guessed they were an enquiry, then a reassurance about the woman's health.

And certainly when the face was turned in her direction Jenni could understand there was no mere formality about the enquiry, for the woman was so obviously unwell. Although there was a certain physical resemblance between the brother and sister, where he had the dark bronzed look of health, her face was pallid, the narrow lips were pulled down as if with pain, and the dark eyes, slightly slanted too with that strange Oriental look, were dull.

But they lit up a little when her brother made the introductions and she held out a hand. 'Miss Cotterell.' She smiled and her face grew brighter. 'How pleased I am to meet you at last!'

Jenni took the thin fingers in hers squeezing them gently to protect their fragility.

'Mrs Kolaios. How are you?'

'At the moment, not so well.' The thin shoulders in the expensive-looking silk dress shrugged. 'This worry with the children . . . But,' she smiled again, 'I'm glad you could come.' The glance she darted at her brother was daring. 'Oh, I know you were opposed to the idea, Peri, but *I'm* glad Miss Cotterell was able to come.' She smiled again at Jenni. 'Do sit down.' Although she spoke good English her accent was much stronger than her brother's and required more concentration. 'Helena will be coming with tea shortly. But tell me,' she waited till her visitor was relaxing in a soft silk upholstered chair, 'how is it that we've never met before? Angela's only sister and we're meeting for the first time.'

Conscious of the hard scrutinising eyes of the man who was lounging against the wall beside the open window, Jenni could not prevent the drift of colour into her cheeks. It was a question she had often asked herself, one to which there was only one answer, but she refused to let Perikles Drimakos know that Angela had never invited her to Greece. 'I don't know either, Mrs Kolaios.' She tried to be casual about the matter. 'I suppose it's because we've seen so little of each other. When Angela has been in London usually she's been rushing off somewhere else. And on this last visit . . .' Abruptly she stopped, unwilling to admit that even then she seemed always to be flying off somewhere else.

'Yes, I suppose so.' Mrs Kolaios sighed. 'That is a pity, I think. Now that I've met you I'm sure of it. You would have been an influence for the better.' She darted a glance at her brother, who was slow to answer her question.

'Yes.' At last he spoke. 'Yes, you are right, of course, Merope. Miss Cotterell would I think have been a sobering influence.'

Jenni glared at him, unable to understand why his

choice of words sounded so patronising. He was, after all, merely echoing his sister's words and she hadn't found those offensive. Then as if to emphasise the inclination his sister spoke again.

'But you aren't at all like Angela.'

'Didn't you know, Mrs Kolaios,' Jenni's voice sounded harsh in her own ears, 'that we aren't really related?' She hoped she was explaining this for the last time. 'My mother married Angela's father when I was a child. My father died when I was a year old. We were brought up as sisters, but that's all. My name was changed when my mother remarried.'

'And her mother?' It was a sharp interjection from the figure by the window.

'Her mother?' Jenni looked at him, not for the moment understanding.

'Angela's mother—was she dead too? At the time of the remarriage?'

'I don't know. No, I think they were divorced.' The direction of his question began to dawn on her and she felt the angry colour rising in her cheeks again, but before she could find some scathing words to answer him the door opened and a young woman came into the room with a tea tray which she put on to a low table beside her mistress's couch. She smiled at Jenni before she withdrew.

'No tea for me.' It was an abrupt, almost brusque comment from the man. 'I see you've had some papers from Vlasos, so I'll just go and have a look at them.' A moment later the door closed behind him.

'You must excuse my brother, Miss Cotterell.' Mrs Kolaios handed a cup across to Jenni. 'He has had a difficult time for the last few months—business worries. Then when he came home the other day and found out that Angela had run off to South America with Giannis following her, then,' she shrugged and smiled, but the smile could not banish the expression of concern in her eyes, 'he almost hit the roof! You see, he gets so angry when the child is simply dumped on me. She is not an easy child, never has been.'

'I know.' Jenni's interruption was instinctive as she remembered the tantrums and tempers which had been features of daily life during their stay in Croydon.

'So, it isn't simply me.' Mrs Kolaios sounded relieved. 'I've often wondered. But the child is so bewildered. She never knows whether her parents will be there in the morning when she wakes up, and . . .'

'Do you mean that this has happened before?'

The older woman stared at Jenni in surprise. 'But don't you know? I'm sorry, my dear, I can see that you don't. I simply assumed that you did. All those times when Angela has run off, sometimes to London, sometimes to the States, I thought her family must know.'

'All I know,' Jenni spoke slowly although her mind was surging with the import of what Mrs Kolaios was saying, 'is that recently Angela and Dina spent a month with me in my flat in Croydon. That's the first real contact I've had with her for several years. Oh, I've had visits from her and Giannis from time to time, brief flying visits, but I had no idea . . .' The deep blue eyes scrutinised the face opposite. 'I'm sorry. I like Giannis so much and I can't understand why . . .' Unable to think of anything comforting to say, her voice trailed away.

'Yes, they are both so young, that is part of the trouble.' Merope Kolaios sighed. 'I just hope that they will both be back soon. But if not both, then at least Giannis.' Her manner hardened slightly. 'You know my brother and my husband were in partnership, Miss Cotterell, and Giannis took over his father's share when Alex died six years ago. But he has paid so little attention that the main burden falls on Peri and it's just too much for him. So I feel guilty when my son fails in his duties, you see. As well as being worried about the marriage.'

'Yes, I see that,' Jenni sighed. 'Of course I'll do everything I can while I'm here, Mrs Kolaios. I understand from your brother that he wants me to take the child to her parents' home in the meantime.'

'That would be best, I think. I really don't feel equal to coping with her, and Magda is unused to children. I wouldn't have asked you to come myself, but at least for that I'm grateful to Angela. Usually she just goes and leaves the child with one of the servants and they in turn bring her to me.' She smiled and a little of the tension left her face. 'I feel happier now that she has someone who might be able to control her. Your being a teacher will help, I think.'

'Yes, I'm sure it will.' Jenni spoke with more confidence than she felt, omitting to state that all her experience and training had been for older children. 'Perhaps I could start her on some lessons.'

'Oh, if you could!' It was a plea. 'I think part of her trouble is boredom. She's an intelligent child underneath all the temper and passion. And if there's anything you want then I hope you'll ring me. When he takes you to the flat Peri will give you my number and show you how to use the telephone. And of course I expect you to bring Dina to see me when you can.'

'Thank you, Mrs Kolaios, I'd like to do that.'

'Oh, please call me Merope. Angela does, and you are so much . . .' the dark eyes travelled over Jenni's features, '. . . so much more my kind of person.' She seemed a little embarrassed as she spoke and it wasn't hard for Jenni to deduce that she had been intending to say that she seemed older. But before she had time to brood on the matter the door opened and Perikles Drimakos came into the room. Quickly his eyes moved from one to the other as if trying to deduce the result of their conversation, and when his sister spoke almost cheerfully his expression relaxed.

'Peri, we've arranged things and I feel much happier now that Jenni is here. I'm sure that at least we shan't have to worry about Dina. She will be in excellent hands. Now all I have to concern me is Giannis—and Angela, of course.' Her brief glance at Jenni was apologetic.

'Good.' As he looked down at his sister Perikles Drimakos actually smiled, momentarily stunning Jenni with the charm of his expression. But the face he turned to her was the other more familiar one. 'Shall we go now, Miss Cotterell?' He glanced at the slim gold watch on his dark wrist. 'I have an appointment later and would like to see you settled in the flat before I leave you.'

'Of course.' Immediately Jenni rose and said a quick goodbye to Merope with a promise that she would telephone soon to let her know how things were progressing.

Then they were walking together down the stairway, the marble of the balustrade cool and smooth under Jenni's fingers. The car journey was completed more or less in silence except for an occasional interruption from Perikles Drimakos, who in a dutiful uninterested voice pointed out one or two places of interest. Jenni made the appreciative noises that were expected of her, but apart from that she said little, and even Dina, who lay against Jenni one thumb comfortingly inserted into her mouth, appeared for once too tired for chatter.

They drove out of the city along the winding coast

road towards Piraeus where Jenni knew that Giannis
and Angela had their flat, and despite the air-condi-
tioning of the car Jenni found herself struggling with
the overwhelming inclination to yawn. Dina gave up
the unequal battle, and by the time the large car
stopped in front of the expensive-looking block her
head had dropped against Jenni's arm and she was
sound asleep.

'That at least is something to be thankful for.' Briefly
Perikles Drimakos smiled at her over the sleeping
form. 'I shall do my best not to disturb her.' When the
car had stopped and they stepped out he bent down
and picked her up, moving with surprising gentleness
so that Dina merely stirred, opened her eyes sleepily,
then settled again into the crook of his arm. 'This way,
Miss Cotterell.' With one powerful shoulder he pushed
open the plate glass door, holding it so that she could
step into the foyer ahead of him. 'Your cases will be
brought up in a moment.'

Behind a desk in the centre of the hall an attendant
stood, and when he recognised the arrivals he came
forward to summon the lift and a moment later they
were being swiftly, smoothly carried to the top floor.
The flat which they entered through the door, opened
by the key her companion took from the pocket of his
jacket, was more like something from an international
magazine than a place where real people stayed.

The hall was enormous, with the extravagant use of
marble which seemed so common in Greece, and she
followed slowly to the bedroom where Dina was put
down on a bed and a light cover was pulled over her.
Then they withdrew and Perikles led the way into a
large kitchen where he pressed a bell and waited with
ill-concealed impatience. At last a door behind them
opened and a middle-aged woman came inside.

'Ah, Gogo,' she was greeted with a frown, 'this is Miss Cotterell. I've brought her and Dina. They will be here until Mr and Mrs Kolaios return.'

'Yes.' The woman smiled and nodded, her eyes travelling with interest over Jenni's by now travel-worn figure.

'The cases are coming up now, Gogo.' Jenni almost smiled at the woman's incongruous name, but the severity of his expression was a powerful deterrent. 'You will see that Miss Cotterell is comfortable while she is here.'

'Yes, sir,' the woman nodded amiably, then hearing someone in the hall went out, presumably to show the chauffeur where to take the cases.

'Through here.' He opened one of the solid-looking doors which matched the array of kitchen cupboards. Jenni followed through a dining-room and into a sit-ting-room which was larger than the whole of the Croydon flat and furnished so exquisitely that she felt her breath was taken away.

'It's so lovely!' She subsided on to one of the soft down-filled chairs, her eyes moving to the display of fine china in a wide display unit and on over a group of delicate watercolours.

'Yes, it's lovely.' He sighed and strolled over to the wide windows which overlooked one corner of the busy harbour and a huge sweep of open sea, now hauntingly beautiful with the setting sun streaking the darkening sky with gold and rose. In silence Jenni watched him reach into a pocket and pull from it a thin black cigar and light it, a match flaring briefly over the dark features. 'Yes, it is lovely, Miss Cotterell—so lovely that you would think that the most fickle woman would be satisfied with it. Add an adoring long-suffering husband and it's hard to believe that even the worst opportunist could have any complaint.'

'Why do you say opportunist?' Jenni fought to retain some self-control as she sat looking up at him. 'Why should you use such an offensive word?'

'Because that's exactly what I believe her to be, Miss Cotterell—a cheap, scheming little opportunist. She was very fortunate indeed that Giannis married her. It was against all the advice of his family and friends, but he insisted and went ahead with it in secret. Oh, your sister was aware of what she was doing all right. Our names are well enough known.'

'In Greece, maybe.' Ice crackled in Jenni's voice. 'But I certainly had heard neither of them. Giannis could have been a waiter in a holiday hotel for all I knew.'

Seeing his lips tighten, she knew that his family pride had been offended and a spasm of satisfaction raced through her. There was something about this man—his arrogance, his condescension, perhaps even the fact that he so firmly disapproved of her being here—that brought out the worst in her. It was good to know that something could ruffle his self-assurance.

'Well, we can leave your opinions out of it, Miss Cotterell. You will simply have to accept my assurance that Angela knew very well what she was doing. You may not have heard the names of Drimakos or Kolaios, but she had. In fact when she came out from England with her bunch of free-wheeling friends she was glad enough to take a job in one of our hotels.'

'Oh?' For the moment Jenni could think of nothing to say; it was obvious he knew so much more about what had happened than she did. All she knew was that Angela had been working in Greece for a year when she had met Giannis and that after a whirlwind romance they had married. She knew that it had been a quiet wedding, which explained why it had been over before she had known about it. And he was implying that his family hadn't been told about it either. Her blue eyes were fixed on that stern remorseless profile as he gazed away from her out towards the horizon.

'Yes, from our point of view, the family's and I'm sure Giannis's too, I think the marriage was a great pity.'

'Well, I don't think it's for you to judge that.' Indignation made her snap at him. 'Perhaps Giannis is perfectly happy. After all, no one forced him to marry Angie.'

The moment she spoke the words Jenni felt a cold trickle down her spine and wished, although she couldn't then understand why, that she could recall them. Perikles Drimakos turned his head and the dark eyes looking at her were brilliant even in the darkness and full of passion.

'But that's exactly what did happen, Miss Cotterell, and I'm sorry if I'm the one to tell you.' He pulled long and slow on his cheroot while he regarded her assessingly. 'Angela was within a month of Dina's birth when they were married. They hadn't seen each other for six months, and if she hadn't reappeared with such opportune suddenness, then all our lives would have been so much easier.'

CHAPTER TWO

IT was ten o'clock that evening before Jenni had time to sit down and think about what Perikles Drimakos had told her; the thunderbolt he had dropped so suddenly had made all colour drain from her face. This was something he must have noticed too, for he took a step towards her, his manner softening as he expressed his concern.

But now of course she couldn't understand why she hadn't guessed. All the indications had been there if she had taken the trouble to notice them: the long periods of silence interspersed by ecstatic letters from Angela, first the wedding news, then almost six months later a note thanking Jenni for her wedding gift and at the same time telling her that a baby was on the way.

By that time, of course, Dina was six months old, and so each time that Jenni sent a birthday gift it was a year out of date. Neither Giannis nor Angela was tall and Dina took after both parents in this respect, so there was nothing about her height in particular which gave any clue to her real age. She was, so Jenni always insisted, very bright for her years, but that was accepted by Angela by a look of smug pride. On the recent visit to London there had even been one occasion when Jenni had corrected Dina, who claimed to be nearly six, and when the confirmation of her age as five had been made by her mother when she returned Jenni assumed that it was just another example of the child's inclination to exaggerate.

Shortly after her uncle had left the flat, Dina had come through to the sitting-room to join her aunt, her face still crumpled by sleep and trailing the cover behind her.

'Come and sit down with me, pet.' Filled with sympathy for the child of such an unhappy alliance, Jenni determined to go out of her way to make her life content, however briefly.

'I'm home!' For almost the first time a smile touched the small face, softening the features that seemed often to have a determination beyond their years. Dina threw herself on to the settee beside Jenni, snuggling against the arm that was put round her. 'Will you tell me a story, Auntie Jen?'

'But I haven't got a book. Do you have some in your cupboards?'

'I don't want a story from a book.' Mutiny, its most usual expression, trembled in the voice. 'I want you to tell me about when you and Mummy were little girls.'

'All right.' Jenni stifled her sigh as she remembered the long involved stories with which she had pacified Dina in Croydon during her mother's frequent absences. But *they* had been told when she was comparatively fresh from a day with twenty teenagers. After her long journey and her session with Perikles Drimakos a day's hard teaching seemed almost like a holiday. She did sigh, quite faintly. Then she began her story.

But at last after they had eaten in the elegant dining room the meal that Gogo had cooked for them, it had been time for Dina to have a bath and be tucked into bed. She demanded another story, but this time agreed to one from her pile of beautifully clean, almost new books written in English and obligingly dropped off to sleep before Jenni had gone very far.

She was crossing the hall from the bedroom to the sitting-room when Gogo stuck her head round the kitchen door.

'Is it all right, Miss Cotterell, that I go upstairs to my flat now?'

'Upstairs?' Jenni looked at her blankly. 'I thought this was the top floor.'

'No.' The older woman smiled and came forward into the hall. 'On the roof Mr Giannis has his garden and there is another tiny flat. I live there with my husband.'

'Of course it's all right, Gogo. You must do just what you do when Mrs Kolaios is here.'

'Only sometimes when she is alone she wishes me to stay downstairs, to sleep in the house.'

'No.' Jenni smiled and shook her head. 'I'm not a bit nervous on my own. I'm used to it, you see. Besides, Dina is with me.'

'Thank you.' Still Gogo hesitated. 'Will Mrs Kolaios be back soon, do you think?'

'I've no idea.'

'Oh.' Clearly the woman was curious and the dark eyes surveyed Jenni frankly. 'It is just that I would like to know when to expect her back, so I can tell the other servants.'

'If I hear then I'll let you know. Are there many other servants?'

'Just two girls, cousins who come in each day. But when Mrs Kolaios is away they usually go to Thessaly to visit their grandmother.'

'You speak excellent English, Gogo.' Jenni tried to change the subject from one which was potentially embarrassing. 'How on earth did you learn?'

The woman, who was short and dark with a tendency to overweight, shrugged her black-clad shoulders. 'It was the war. I worked for the British when they were here and after I used to listen to the B.B.C. Then when Mrs Kolaios came I was working in one of the cafés on the front and she persuaded me to come and work for her. We were having trouble finding a house to live in at the time, so my husband agreed, although he didn't at first like the idea. But it has all been for the best and we are quite happy.' She paused. 'Mr and Mrs Kolaios have been very kind to us.'

'And of course,' Jenni could not stop herself confirming what she already knew, 'Mrs Kolaios speaks no Greek.'

'No.' The rather full lips were pursed, the shoulders shrugged again expressively. 'That is a pity. I have tried to persuade her to learn, but she seems to close her mind to it. It is as if she's afraid of failure so refuses to try. But then no one can pretend that it is an easy language.'

'So she has you to tell the other servants what to do.'

'That, and the shopping. But I don't mind. I enjoy it. Besides, who would not enjoy working in such beautiful surroundings?' Gogo unconsciously echoed words that had been spoken earlier. 'When I feel fed-up I sometimes come down and just look round the rooms. You have seen the entire flat, Miss Cotterell?'

'No, not all of it. But what I have seen is beautiful. The room I have . . .'

'Oh, I forgot to say that I took your things out of the cases. I was afraid of them being creased. They are hanging in the wardrobe and some are in the drawers.'

'Thank you.' Jenni blushed when she thought of her clothes which she had meant to unpack for herself. She wondered what Gogo had thought of the drab selection of dresses and the simple underclothes. They must be

as far from Angela's couture clothes as it was possible
to be. She turned again towards the sitting-room with
an impatient little gesture. 'That was kind of you. But
I won't keep you any longer. Goodnight, Gogo.'

'Goodnight. I shall be down for your breakfast and
if there's anything you want me to do you can let me
know then.'

Jenni walked through to the sitting room, pulled one
of the large softly upholstered armchairs up to the huge
windows overlooking the lights of the harbour, and sat
down, closing her eyes and with a sigh of relief and
kicked off the flat sandals she had been wearing all day.

Her mind was a jumble—impressions, anxieties,
prejudices, all crowding in on her so that the calm self-
contained Miss Cotterell from the staff room at St
Ermyn's didn't know whether she was coming or
going. But everything about this situation was a contradiction, from the precipitate way she had made up
her mind in response to Angela's telephone call,
brushing aside not only the headmaster's protestations
but Jeremy's as well. Poor Jeremy! Her lips curved
into a faint smile. It was such a shock for him to find
her so intransigent—that was the word he had used.

'It's not like you to be so intransigent, love.'

And it had been. Unlike her. Usually she and Jeremy
saw eye to eye on everything. It was just this one
thing—because Angela sounded so desperate. And she
had never asked her to do anything else. At least, not
something big like this. Other smaller things, yes, as
Jeremy had so rightly pointed out.

'She makes use of you, you do realise that, don't
you, Jenni? For months not a word. Last Christmas
not even a card. Then without even asking if it's all
right she moves in with you, she and the child.'

'Well, she has no one else. If we had parents then

we'd both be imposing on them, I suppose.'

'You're too goodnatured, that's all. And you had to babysit every blessed night. Where did she get to, that's what I'd like to know?'

And that was something that Jenni would have liked to know. Then, during the time Angela had spent in the flat, but even more since Perikles Drimakos with scarcely concealed suspicion had asked the very same question in the room she was now sitting in.

And when she had explained diffidently, with just a shade of unwilling apology in her voice, that although Angela had gone out from time to time in the evenings—she hadn't dared say just how often—she had never said exactly where she was going, the anger which had been smouldering in him had almost exploded.

'So,' he had almost hissed the words at her, 'your sister used to go out in the evenings but you didn't know where. She didn't tell you and you didn't ask. All you did was look after the child for her, release her from her duties so that she could follow any path she fancied. What time of night did she come home, Miss Cotterell?'

Jenni felt her cheeks suddenly flame, but she looked him straight in the eye and answered calmly, denying the fury that made her want to lash out at him. 'I don't know what time she came in at nights. It wasn't really my business.'

'Not your business!' His explosive anger was under control now but his eyes were mercilessly scathing. 'She is your younger sister, pretty, scatterbrained—to put it at its most innocent—and you think nothing of it if she goes traipsing about a city like London till all the hours!'

'I don't know if you appreciate the situation, Mr

Drimakos. I was out doing a full day's work, coming
home to clean my flat, usually making a meal for myself
and Dina and often enough for my fiancé too.' In her
anger she disregarded that fact that strictly speaking
she and Jeremy were not engaged. 'By the time I got
to bed at night I was tired. Tired, Mr Drimakos!' She
tossed her head at him, allowed her eyes to flash, and
if she had thought about it she might have wondered if
she ought to be enjoying her rôle quite so much. 'So
tired that I would fall asleep when my head touched
the pillow. I had no energy for sitting up with a stop-
watch in my hand, waiting for your nephew's wife to
come back home.' When she stopped she was slightly
breathless and even wondered if she had in her excitement got mixed up with that last relationship. She tried
to remember what she had said, but while she was
doing so he spoke again in a voice so cold that she
shivered even while she couldn't understand where his
question was leading.

'Was Wimbledon on when Angela was in London?'

'Wimbledon?' Blankly she gazed back into the
intense face. 'Do you mean . . .'

'Tennis, Miss Cotterell, that's what I mean. Was the
Wimbledon Championship on when she was with you?'

'Yes.' There was a flash in Jenni's mind and she was
back in the flat at Croydon laughing at the intense, the
feverish excitement Angela had shown when they were
watching one of the first round matches on an outside
court. 'Do you know this Ramon Perez, Angela?' She
recalled saying those very words which made her reaction to Perikles Drimakos's use of the name a guilty
start.

'Have you heard of Ramon Perez?' His eyes narrowed. 'I see you have, and I don't need to ask where you
heard it.'

During the long pause while they stared at each other, Jenni could hear her heart beating very loudly. 'Do you mean . . .?' She couldn't complete the question.

'Yes, of course that is what I mean.' He had turned angrily away from her then. 'Angela has run off to South America in pursuit of this latest in a long line— an ageing tennis professional.' He made a gesture of disgust. 'You didn't think she had run away to South America to study the culture? No one who ever knew her could possibly think that.'

'Don't . . .' the words burst from her lips, 'don't speak of her as if she were dead!' She waited for a reply, but when none came she went on more calmly.

'I'm sorry about what has happened, Mr Drimakos. As I told you earlier, I like Giannis, although I've met him only three times when he and Angie have paid brief visits to London. I had no idea that there were problems—they always seemed so happy. And if it's all as you say,' in spite of the quenching expression on his face she forced herself to meet his gaze, 'I feel sure there must be some reason for it. I don't think Angela would behave like that without a motive.' But at the back of her mind was the recollection of erratic behaviour stretching over the years. 'In any case,' even although her courage was failing she determined to defend herself from his outrageous accusations, 'I resent being held responsible. I've seen very little of Angela since she married. If, as you say, this is not the first time such a thing has happened then I think you should look to your own family.' She ignored the flashing anger of his eyes. 'As I wasn't here on those other occasions I can hardly be held responsible for them. Just as I refuse to be blamed for this present situation.'

For a long time they glared at each other, but in the end it was Perikles Drimakos who turned away. 'I see that this is a matter on which we shall never agree, so there is no point in talking about it any further. I only ask you, Miss Cotterell, if your sister should telephone you at some time, please do not try to persuade her to come home. I tried unsuccessfully to insist that Giannis should leave her alone, but he *would* rush off to plead with her to return to her home and her duty. As he has done so often in the past, as by now she expects him to do.'

'As you so obviously disapprove of her then perhaps that's one of the reasons why she's been so unhappy.'

'I think you overrate her sensitivity. In any case, at the beginning she was warmly received into the family. It was only later that things changed. That's why I'm asking you not to interfere.'

'But you must leave me to decide what I should say to Angela when she rings. I can't agree to do just what suits you, before I've even heard her version of things.' Her lips felt taut and disapproving.

'I can't force you, of course. I only feel that it would perhaps be less painful in the end if . . .'

'What you mean is that you'd like to be relieved of the problem!' Jenni flared angrily at him. 'You would trample people's feelings under foot just so long as you can have things fixed to suit you. It must be very nice, Mr Drimakos, to be so rich, so powerful that you can fix anything that upsets you.' When she had spoken Jenni held her breath, wishing that her anxiety to strike back at him hadn't persuaded her to say too much. She imagined she saw him struggle for control, but his voice when at last he spoke was even, almost dispassionate.

'Yes, I suppose in some ways it is. I hadn't thought of it much. But don't run away with the idea that money can buy whatever you want, Miss Cotterell. From my own experience I can tell you that is very far from the truth.'

Then almost without pausing for breath he had changed the subject completely, speaking to her as if they hadn't just had the most fiery conversation; mentioning things that she would be most likely to have difficulty with in the days ahead. Finally, with a courteous goodnight, he had left, and Jenni found herself totally exhausted, but at the same time stimulated, exhilarated in a way that she hadn't been for years.

The following days passed quietly enough, they might even have been dull if it hadn't been for the fact that Jenni saw everything about the great port as exciting and stimulating. Even Dina, seeming to find some satisfaction in the role of guide, was more docile than she had been in London. Which wasn't to say that she was all at once transformed from fiend to angel, rather that she settled down somewhere in between the two extremes.

Jenni spoke daily to Mrs Kolaios on the telephone and one day made the journey by bus from Piraeus into Athens and then by taxi up to the villa. When they reached the gates Dina insisted on being held up so that she could ring the bell, then speak to Magda asking in Greek, with what sounded remarkably like politeness, if they could be allowed inside to visit.

Merope, Jenni now knew, had a rare blood disorder and was much the same as before, although on this visit she was downstairs in the large salon which had french windows thrown open to a vine-shaded terrace. She had a piece of canvas work in her hands which every so often she took up from the sofa, did a few stitches, then let it drop on to her lap again as if she were exhausted.

'So.' Her smile at Jenni was wan. 'You have worked a miracle on the child.'

'No.' But in spite of her denial a tiny shred of pride was irresistible. 'She's not always as quiet as this by any means.' Together they looked out on to the terrace where Dina was frowning over an attempt to write something in a book she had brought with her. 'But I have found that she's quite keen to learn to write. The last two days we've been doing a little before lunch. Of course all I can teach is English, but I think it's time she started school. Even a nursery class would help her.'

'Yes. But Angela said she wasn't ready.' The dark eyes that were so like her brother's turned to look at Jenni. 'Have you heard anything?'

'From Angela? No, nothing.' She looked questioningly at the other woman.

'I had a call from Giannis last night, but he said very little. Just that he had seen Angela and they were discussing matters. He seemed relieved when I told him that you had come to take care of Dina for a little while. I hope that at last they can get things sorted out.' Merope sighed.

Jenni was on the verge of expressing some comforting opinion, but then decided to hold her tongue. What right had she to say anything of the kind when Angela had behaved so abominably? In spite of her refusal to accept what he had said about it until she had had confirmation, she was fairly well assured that what Perikles Drimakos had told her about Angela wasn't far from the truth.

Instead she began to talk about sewing, asking to be

allowed to look at the piece of embroidery and then studying the seat cover with real interest.

'I've always been meaning to do something like this, but somehow there never seems to be the time,' she told Merope.

'I started on these before I was married. Before you go you must ask Magda to let you see my dining room. I worked all the chair seats in there.' Merope screwed up her face slightly and laughed. 'Twelve ordinary dining chairs and two carvers. I often wonder that I ever embarked on such a task!'

'It must have taken years.' There was something about Merope which made Jenni feel very gentle. In fact the emotions she engendered were quite the opposite of the ones her brother seemed to produce. 'But what a legacy to leave behind you! And this one?' She held up the long piece of canvas. 'This is for something else?'

'Yes. I meant it for the children's wedding anniversary. It's a long fender stool and it has taken me more than a year. But what's the use,' she reached out her thin hand and took it from Jenni so that it could be rolled up and put aside, 'maybe there will never be any need to finish it . . .' She bit her lower lip feverishly, but fortunately just at that moment Dina came running in with the piece of paper, her name in large slightly sprawling letters written across it. Her face was scarlet with the effort of concentration, her manner when she handed the paper to her grandmother a mixture of diffidence and pride.

For a few moments they spoke to each other in Greek, then Merope with a faint apologetic smile at Jenni continued the congratulations in English. Later in the afternoon they had tea on the terrace, and when it was time to go Merope insisted that they should be taken back home by her gardener.

While they drove back to Piraeus Dina chattered incessantly, but Jenni's replies were slightly distracted, for she realised that what she had been hoping for during the visit to the villa had not been achieved. This in spite of the fact that once or twice she had given the conversation a nudge in the general direction she wanted it to go. Any reference by his sister to Perikles Drimakos had been brief and casual, wholly unsatisfying for her listener and giving no real clue about the private life of the man. Still she didn't know if he were married, Jenni reminded herself. Then she wondered why she should even be interested in such a thing. Not that she was—not really. It was simply that he was such a powerful personality one could hardly help being curious, that was all.

Two nights later and she was almost at the end of her first week in Greece but still without having heard anything from Angela. She couldn't say that she was lonely, for Gogo was usually available to talk to and when they went shopping Dina was surprisingly good company. She still had tantrums, but fortunately was becoming less inclined to make them public and no longer had them in the streets as she had been in the habit of doing in Croydon. They had settled down into a routine which seemed to have a calming effect on them all.

'Will you read me that story about the Minotaur tonight, Auntie Jen?' the little girl begged.

'The Minotaur?' Jenni, who was squeezing some shampoo on to her hand while she knelt on the floor by Dina's bath, laughed. 'Now close your eyes in case you get some of it in your eyes, darling.' She splashed water on to the soft dark hair and began to rub the soap on to it. 'That's a strange story for a little girl.

I'm not even sure I know it properly.'

'Yes, you do.' There was a wail of protest in Dina's voice as she screwed her eyes tight shut. 'Everyone knows the story.'

'Hang on a moment while I begin to rinse you.' Using the spray Jenni began to wash away the soap. 'There now. That's better. Can you hear it squeak? That's how you know it's clean.' She took one of the soft pink towels and wrapped a turban round the child's head. 'Now are you ready to come out of the bath?'

'Only when you promise to tell me about the Minotaur.' Dina's eyebrows were drawn together in a determined frown.

'Well, I'll see. I don't remember seeing that story in any of your books. And I'm not sure that it's a proper story for a little girl.'

'Oh, it is.' Dina grinned showing a gap where one of her front teeth had fallen out. 'It's all about this monster, and he has to eat seven young men and seven maidens every year.'

'Oh dear!' Jenni shivered fearfully. 'I don't like the sound of him at all. Maybe you should tell me the story, since you know so much about it.'

'Oh, Auntie Jen!' Immediately the small face began to pout. 'That isn't fair! You promised.'

'I did no such thing.' Jenni laughed and putting her hands beneath Dina's arms she lifted her from the water, enveloping her in a huge towel. 'I said that I'd see.'

'O-o-oh!' It was suspiciously like the beginning of a tantrum. 'You're *hurting* me, you know.'

'I think the best thing would be for me to tell you the story of the Minotaur.' Perikles Drimakos's deep tones came from the open door, making them both turn to look at the tall figure lounging against the lintel. The dark eyes flicked over Dina, then came to rest on Jenni, who was at once made conscious of her steam-damp hair and the way her tee-shirt was clinging stickily. Sulkily she wondered if he had chosen the pale grey suit and red tie specially to provide a contrast to her own casual shirt and jeans. Even his brown calf slip-on shoes, so perfectly polished, seemed to mock her.

'Uncle Peri!' Was the child's voice actually signalling pleasure at the unexpected arrival?

'Mr Drimakos.' Her own would surely disabuse him that any pleasure was shared by her.

'Miss Cotterell.' There was something peculiar about their formality which must have accounted for the sudden lightening of her spirits, but there was no answering spark of amusement in his eyes and almost at once he transferred his attention to his niece. 'So if you will agree I shall tell you the story of the Minotaur when you are safely tucked up in bed. And while you and I are busy with that I'm sure Miss Cotterell will welcome a break, because I'd like to have a word with her. I have an important proposition to put to her.' The shining tilted eyes flicked up at her again, challenging and very dark.

CHAPTER THREE

DINA was safely tucked beneath the bedcovers, her hair dry, shining and clean, tied back from her forehead by a dark red ribbon, listening wide-eyed to her uncle's calm voice before Jenni managed to get away and to lean in sudden exhaustion on the door of her bedroom. While she tried to recover from the sudden unexpected appearance of the man who had been so much in her thoughts since she had met him, her eyes moved restlessly about the room.

Even after a week she still felt a thrill of pleasure each time she entered and sometimes a pang as she thought of the inevitable approach of the time when she must leave. And it went without saying that she would never again occupy a room that was half as lovely. The pale cream walls provided a perfect background for the flower prints, glowing with soft subtle shades, making such an eye-catching group on one wall. That they had been no casual choice was illustrated in the way the deep rose was picked up in the silk of bedcover and curtains, a brilliant blue in the small velvet-upholstered armchair drawn up by the window and in the thick carpet the colour of sage.

Her eyes moved quickly to the door of the bathroom, which stood slightly open giving a glimpse of the cream ceramic suite and Japanese wallpaper, handpainted with roses and exotic birds. When she had first seen it it had occurred to Jenni that surely only Angela would be so extravagant as to use handpainted wallpaper in a bathroom, but even in so short a time she was beginning to take such things for granted.

But at this moment she paid little attention to what normally gave so much pleasure. She was trying to think what she had in her wardrobe, something that would not make Perikles Drimakos raise his usual critical eyebrow. She could of course simply brazen it out—run a quick brush through her hair and go back into the sitting-room still wearing the jeans and tee-shirt she had had on since lunch time. But something, the woman in her, longed for an outfit that was pretty and feminine.

Then she remembered a dress which she had pushed into a plastic bag in her case at the last moment and which was still lying, unwrapped, in one of the shelf compartments of the huge wardrobe. She went and shook it out, blessing whoever had invented polyester fabric when she saw it unfurl into a creaseless simple shape.

It took her less than ten minutes to get ready, for she quickly ripped off what she was wearing, leaving her things in a pile on the bathroom floor before slipping into a pair of panties and pulling the dress down over her suntanned shoulders. She shook back the mane of auburn hair from her forehead, feeling freer now that she had released it from its usual band, and turned to study her reflection.

Remembering the only other time she had tried on the dress, she again wondered at Jeremy's reaction. Jenni had chosen it from an illustration in one of the glossy colour supplements and had been surprised at the immediate dislike he had taken to it. Perhaps there was, as he had said, something cheap about it. Or maybe it was the greyer English skies made one think so. Here, its creamy colour with narrow lines of navy and yellow looked suitable enough, as did the style.

The tie shoulders showed a great deal of skin, besides revealing that it was impossible to wear a bra with it, but plenty of the girls in Piraeus were wearing much less.

Could it be what she had thought at the time, that Jeremy didn't like the idea of other men seeing her wearing it? Her wide lips curved into a tender smile at the idea. If only she could believe that he was jealous, as Jean had said!

She had been trying it on when Jean had come running down from the flat upstairs, just in time to hear Jeremy's damning comment.

'Don't let him have all his own way. He's probably jealous. It's amazing how the average Englishman would like to shut his woman away so that nobody else can look at her. You take my word for it, love, and keep the dress, you look fabulous in it. You know what they say on the telly,' she showed her teeth in what was meant to be a wolfish grin, 'if you've got it, flaunt it.' She growled deep down in her throat, laughed at Jeremy's expression, clutched the packet of tea to her and made for the door.

Jeremy's face had shown too clearly his reaction to the incident. 'You let everyone impose on you,' he grumbled.

'Nonsense!' Jenni had twisted, trying to see the rear view of the dress in the mirror over the mantelpiece. 'I'll get the tca back. Besides, I borrowed two eggs from her last week when I found I'd run out.' She paused. 'You don't like it, then?'

'Not really.' He had shaken his copy of the *Guardian* which he always brought with him, applying himself to the leading article with great diligence. 'You can get your money back, can't you?'

'Yes,' Jenni had sighed, 'I suppose so. Only it's such

a fag wrapping it all up again.' Still, she *had* meant to do it. Only some perverse feeling of annoyance had kept her from the sensible course until too late. But now it seemed a piece of luck that she had kept the dress, and that she had brought it with her.

Hastily she thrust her bare feet into high heelless sandals, the only ones she had that increased her height. Since she and Jeremy were almost of a size she had the tendency to choose flatties, but she had a suspicion that this evening some extra inches would be a positive benefit.

It was the work of an instant to apply the merest trace of bronze shadow to her eyelids, to smooth some gold blusher on her cheekbones and to run a brush through her hair. Then she was ready; she had no intention of allowing him to think that she had gone to a great deal of trouble simply for him. She whirled away from her image, angry that she should even harbour such a thought, and walked over the marble tiling of the hall and into the sitting room.

He was sitting on the edge of a chair, and she sensed that getting to his feet was an instinct rather than a response to her as a woman. Nevertheless she knew that he was seeing her for the first time, the eyes swept over her, noting the loose shining waves of her hair, the bare golden shoulders and the narrow belted waist. Her heart gave a curious jolt.

'You would like a drink.' Without waiting for an answer he turned from her and she watched while he busied himself at the cabinet which held glasses and bottles and was always stocked with ice and slices of orange and lemon. When he turned she was sitting on the sofa, her slim legs crossed so that her bare toes, the nails painted shiny pink, could scarcely be avoided. Once again, quite irrationally, Jenni told herself, she blessed the boredom which last night had led her to give herself a manicure and pedicure.

'Thank you.' She put out a hand to take the drink that he offered, their fingers momentarily touching round the cool glass and ridiculously bringing colour into her cheeks. He hadn't asked what she would like, but when she tasted the mixture of vermouth and soda which she had seen him concoct, savoured the additional flavours of bitters and a twist of lemon, she couldn't withhold her appreciation.

'Mmm.' She searched in a small drawer for some drip mats and put her glass down on one, placing another on the table in front of his chair. 'Nice—refreshing!' As she spoke her eye caught sight of the letter she had received that morning from Jeremy. It was lying with the address turned round so that Perikles could read it. She knew that it had been turned round deliberately, and she looked up to find his eyes on her, in his hand a drink to match her own.

He made no attempt to evade the question he saw in her expression. 'You have heard from England?'

'Yes.' She refused to acknowledge the warmth in her cheeks. 'I had a letter this morning—from my fiancé,' she added with a touch of defiance.

'I see.' He slumped into the chair opposite, studying her through those curious eyes that held no hint of friendship. 'What is his name?'

'His name,' she spoke with great patience, 'is Jeremy Brown.' Although it's none of your business, her tone informed him clearly.

'Jeremy.' As he spoke the name it seemed to Jenni that there was a world of condescension in it, yet she couldn't repress the disloyal thought that it seemed callow, unsophisticated and utterly English.

'Perikles.' Her voice was a mocking parody of his

own. 'It sounds as if you spend your time taking thorns out of lions' feet.'

'Alas,' he finished his drink at a gulp and sat staring, tapping his glass idly against his hand so that the ice clinked, 'I've never had occasion to do that Miss Cotterell. Unlike Androcles.'

This time there was no escaping the embarrassing wave of scarlet that under his impassive gaze swept over her. How could she have been such a fool? But before she could find an answer to that interesting question she realised he was asking her another question.

'And what does he do? Jeremy, I mean.' He spoke with conscious sarcasm.

'He's a social worker.'

'Oh, I see.' The disdain was there again.

'He's fiercely committed to his clients, of course.'

'Of course. I get the idea.' He pulled a thin black cheroot from his pocket and lit it, blowing the smoke negligently to one side. 'People sit round in groups and talk about their problems.'

'How easy for you to sneer!'

'Was I?' He raised a disdainful eyebrow. 'I don't think I meant to. Let's say that you should be less touchy about your fiancé's occupation.'

'O-o-oh!' It was an interjection remarkably like Dina's when she was on the threshold of losing her temper, and at the same time Jenni put down her empty glass with a bump and stood up. 'I'd better go and see if Dina's all right.'

'There's no need. She was almost asleep when I left her and I'm sure she would have let us know by this time if she had still been awake.'

'Nevertheless,' Jenni answered coldly, 'I prefer to check for myself.'

Somewhat to her annoyance when she went into Dina's room the child was lying, sleeping soundly, the thumb of one hand comfortingly in her mouth. Gently Jenni removed the thumb, bent down and kissed her soft cheek and moved to the door. But on her way she paused, her attention caught by her own reflection, struck by the flush in her cheeks and the shining excitement in her eyes. Confounded by such a contradictory sight, she made a quick grimace before reaching for the switch which dimmed the bedroom lights.

'Would you care to eat with me?' Standing in the doorway, she addressed her question to Perikles in a rebellious tone which was quite at variance with the one she intended to use. 'Gogo,' her use of the name was intended to remind him how ridiculous that sounded, 'left a cold meal for me, and there's enough for two.' She found that she was holding her breath while she waited for him to answer.

'No, thank you,' he stretched his arm and looked at his wrist watch. 'I have an engagement this evening. But come and sit down, please, Miss Cotterell, we still have something to discuss. And we must not allow ourselves to be so easily diverted by your tendency to lose your temper.'

She would have liked to refuse, to tell him that she had waited long enough for her supper and that she would prefer to eat now, but some compulsion, the power of his personality perhaps, made her walk over the floor and sit down in her original position facing him.

'Dina was all right?' His tone was surprisingly mild.

'Yes. She was asleep—as you said she would be.' It was impossible to keep the sarcasm from her voice. 'Perhaps we can get on, Mr Drimakos.' Now she was suggesting that she had a hundred things she must do. 'You said you had something to discuss with me. A proposition, I think you called it.'

'Yes.' His voice was as cool as the ice melting in her glass. 'It was not my idea, Miss Cotterell, but my sister's really. So whatever your reaction I trust that you will save it for her.'

Jenni stared, unable to imagine what was to come next.

'You have heard nothing from Angela?'

Without speaking she shook her head.

'And Merope has heard only once from Giannis. But,' his eyes were boring into her, 'today I managed to contact him through a friend in Mexico and it seems,' he paused and when he spoke again there was a cynical note in his voice, 'it seems that Giannis has every hope that things can be smoothed out. Needless to say, when he told me that I let him know my own feelings.'

'Naturally.' If her repeated sarcasm annoyed him for once he concealed it.

'But the line to Mexico was excruciating and I don't think the force of my opinion got over to him. In any case I doubt if they will be back in less than ten days, and so . . .'

'And so . . .' Her eyes were riveted on his face and she tried to ignore the way her heart felt as if it were being squeezed from her body. Ten days, she thought. Only ten more days.

'I am going on a short cruise round the Cyclades and would like you and Dina to come with us.'

'A cruise?' Jenni could scarcely believe that she had heard him speak the words.

'Yes. I own a boat which seems to spend all its time tied up at the quayside. I find that I can get away for about a week, so I would like you to come, Miss Cotterell.' He stood up with the air of having done what he had been told to do and now waited for her decision.

'When . . .' she ran the tip of her tongue round her dry lips, 'when are you leaving?'

'That's the trouble—although why it should be one, I don't know.' He gave the impression of patience sorely tried. 'We are leaving at midday tomorrow. There's no reason why you shouldn't be ready in time. All you need is a bag with some casual clothes.' His glance seemed to tell her that that should pose no problem. 'Oh, and don't forget some swimming things, for you and for the child.'

He stood waiting for his answer and as she said nothing he went on with a touch of irritability, 'My sister is very grateful for what you have done for Dina.' His expression told her clearly enough that she needn't think he was.

'Thank you.' She sounded pert and ungracious and she had the satisfaction of seeing his eyes narrow. 'And the cruise is to be a reward for me, is that it?'

'If you like to think of it in that way.' The broad shoulders beneath the fine grey suiting shrugged expressively. 'I prefer to think of it as an expression of gratitude. You took over in what was a difficult situation, and from the little I've seen of Dina it seems you've done a good job.'

In a swift movement contrived to hide the brilliance of the tears that suddenly stung her eyes Jenni turned away to look unseeingly at the slow progress of a few lights across the water.

'Thank you.' Her voice was dull and lifeless. 'I would like to come.'

'Good.' She had no idea whether he was pleased by

her acceptance or not, but in the dark glass she saw him look again at his watch. 'Then someone will collect you just before midday tomorrow. Don't bring too much stuff. So goodnight, Miss Cotterell.'

'Goodnight.' Feeling more in control of herself, she turned again to look at him. 'I shall look forward to it.'

But when she was alone in the large flat she questioned the sense that had made her accept his totally unexpected invitation. It was so clear that it had been issued unwillingly. She could just imagine the little scene at the villa which had led up to it—Merope telling him what a wonderful job Jenni was doing, hinting that it might be a good thing to reward her in some way, suggesting that as he was going on a short cruise ... His unwillingness ... A little pleading, cajolery. After all, it will be for just a few days. Quite soon the children will be back and she will have to return to London. Poor thing, she has this dreary boy-friend ... It will be something for her to look back on ...

Angry with herself, Jenni pressed her hands to her head and groaned. What was wrong with her? She wasn't usually so sorry for herself. Why should the invitation be anything other than it appeared to be, a very pleasant gesture to a visitor? Why should she feel so uptight and huffy about it simply because it had been her sister's idea, not his? And why, come to that, did they so often seem to be scratchy with each other? She didn't usually go about looking for slights, for hidden meanings in whatever was said to her. But that was how she was with Perikles Drimakos. She had even made that ghastly remark about his name—her skin crept at the very recollection.

Firmly she threw her head back and went into the dining room. She was hungry, that's what it was. And the glass of vermouth might have been more potent than she had thought. On an empty stomach too. Gloomily she piled her plate with the cold meat and added some avocado salad, turning her eyes away from the small carafe of wine left so temptingly beside her place. She hoped that she hadn't shown any sign of intoxication in front of him. That would be the very last straw.

Doggedly she ate her way through the food, scarcely noticing the delicious sweetness of the goat's milk cheese which had been left in a covered dish and eating the perfectly ripe peach without interest. When she had finished she pushed her chair back, collected her dirty crockery and walked with it through to the kitchen. In spite of what Gogo said she had no intention of leaving everything until tomorrow; having once shared a flat with a girl who never washed up behind her she knew how very irritating that could be.

It took only a few moments to wash the few things and put everything tidily back into the cupboards, then she made a cup of instant coffee and took it through to the sitting-room. For a long time she stood in front of the huge windows, looking out rather aimlessly at the strings of lights below her, watching the speeding headlights of cars as they made their way swiftly along the waterfront before disappearing on their secret errands. The lights in the harbour rose and fell gently with the water, and stirring her coffee, Jenni wondered idly which of those hundreds of boats was his.

She still could hardly believe it—that she, Jenni Cotterell, would tomorrow be sailing round the Greek islands on a millionaire's yacht! It was almost worth having risked her job—and her pension—for such a once in a lifetime's opportunity. She raised the coffee cup to her lips, wrinkling her nose when she realised that it was almost cold, then swallowing the rest quickly as if it was a glass of medicine.

But now she thought she'd better go and try to decide what she was going to take with her. There were several things she must do tomorrow; she would have to exchange some of her travellers' cheques and she really ought to answer Jeremy's letter to let him know that she would be away for a few days, which would leave little time for packing.

Jenni felt almost cheerful as she threw open the wardrobe door, and even the sight of so many neutral colours was scarcely enough to depress her, although it did serve to remind her that when she got home she was going to adopt a different attitude to clothes buying. She would concentrate on her own likes and dislikes and forget about other people's. Firmly she guided her mind away from any exact definition of 'other people'. Disloyalty could go only so far, and it was impossible to compare Perikles Drimakos with . . . other people.

But thinking of him did concentrate her mind on one fact. During the week that they would be thrown together in close contact she determined that she would go out of her way to be pleasant to him. She didn't care for the knowledge that he must already have the idea that she was an extremely awkward woman. Jenni smiled faintly to herself as she took a pink denim skirt from a hanger and laid it on the bed with a few other things that needed a rub from an iron. His experience with Angela had probably inclined him towards a prejudiced impression of Englishwomen, and it wasn't necessary to reinforce that.

She would, she promised herself, be so sweet and amenable that he would be taken completely by surprise and might even begin to wonder why initially he had had such a low opinion of her. It was just conceivable that they could find they had something in common. Clearly he was concerned about his nephew, and equally she was worried about Angela. She preferred to draw a veil over his barely concealed wish that the marriage should come to an end. That could have been something said in a moment's exasperation and not to be taken entirely seriously.

Jenni, aware of an unusual sound, stopped in the midst of her efficient smoothing folding operation and stood for a moment, her head tilted to one side as she listened. Then she laughed aloud at her own foolishness for what she had heard was her own voice. She had been singing softly beneath her breath, that had been the unusual sound which had intruded into her muted excitement.

She must try to get her emotions under control. She was fully aware that since she had arrived in Athens Perikles Drimakos had been exercising an influence on her life quite unjustified by anything that had passed between them. Deprived of any kind of stimulating company, she had taken to daydreaming about him. In other words, she had been thinking of him because she had had little else to think about. And possibly the fact that their dislike had been so instant and so mutual had coloured her impression of him.

Anyway, now that she had decided on a new approach, he would fade naturally to a proper place in her thoughts. And naturally Jeremy would regain his. For, and she hated to admit it, he had been in great danger of being displaced.

After a moment or two sitting on the side of her bed thinking such sensible thoughts Jenni remembered that moment when he had handed the drink to her. The touch of his hand on hers had been like an electric current passing between them. At the time it had been totally unexpected, and yet not in the least surprising.

It was interesting to remember that for a split second she imagined that mirrored on his face she had seen a reflection of her own feelings, but it vanished so quickly that she decided it was a result of the day-dreams which had been afflicting her for the last few days. Either that or it was quite simply an expression of his distaste at having to come into actual physical contact with her. For a moment Jenni's look of dreamy amusement faltered, then she shook her head in disbelief.

'What on earth is the matter with you, Jenni?' She spoke aloud using the tone normally reserved for abstracted dewy-eyed girls during classes. 'You're behaving like a teenager!'

Now! She jumped up with a determination to avoid thinking about Perikles Drimakos any longer. A swimming suit. It was just by chance she was a good swimmer and that she and Jeremy had spent a week last summer diving to a wreck off the Cornish coast. The black swimsuit she had worn then was functional, businesslike, and was still rolled up in one of the pockets inside her case.

It took no more than a moment to retrieve it and shake it out. It would be, she decided, the first time such a costume had been worn on a yacht like the one she would be on, but at least when she wore it, Perikles Drimakos would be unlikely to give her a second glance. But if Jenni expected the thought to be a comfort why should it have quite the opposite effect? Why should she feel as if a rug had suddenly been pulled out from under her feet?

CHAPTER FOUR

QUITE simply she could have imagined nothing so perfect as this effortless slipping out of the harbour, the sprawl of buildings along the coastline gradually diminishing until they became a smear finally vanishing in a shimmer of white and green. The breeze, warm, soporific, drove them on effortlessly, up the coastline through the heavenly blue of the sea, towards the matching colour of the sky on a distant horizon.

Jenni leaned forward into the wind, her eyes behind dark glasses closed as she felt the cool sea air blowing through her hair, whipping the thin cotton of her dress close to her body. Her ears were filled by the soft rush of the air so that she failed to hear him approach.

'Welcome aboard, Miss Cotterell.'

'Mr Drimakos.' Her eyes shot open as she half-turned to find him leaning against the rail beside her, the dark eyes watching her intently. She had no idea how long he had been standing there and she was grateful for the slight protection given by the smoked glass. Feeling his appraising glance take in each detail of her appearance, she could not control the blush that spread over her skin.

'I'm sorry I could not come to see you earlier. As you will understand,' his smile was a flash of white in his sun-browned face, 'I was busy leaving harbour.'

'Of course.' It was a pleasure to be able to return his smile, to let her eyes linger on the handsome face, now much more relaxed than she had seen it before.

57

Perhaps that was the effect of his casual clothes, for he
was wearing a pair of navy linen slacks and thrust
inside them a white shirt, open to the waist, revealed a
distracting amount of dark skin and curling black hair.
'Of course.' She repeated the words, unable to think of
anything else at the moment, and turned to her original
position, which was much less disturbing. 'I . . .' she
began, but stopped when at the same time he spoke.

'Paul and Sofia picked you up all right?'

'Yes, thank you. And I was so pleased that they
brought Panos with them. I left Dina with him down
in the cabin. She greeted him like a long-lost brother—
although,' she laughed as she glanced round at him,
'he was less enthusiastic!'

'I can imagine.' She felt his eyes on her profile as
he answered. 'Of course there's two years' age difference, as well as the male assumption of superiority . . .'
He paused and she knew that he was challenging her to
comment, a challenge she could hardly resist.

'So long as you admit that it's simply an assumption.'

'Of course.' His gentle mockery was a pleasant sensation and she wondered if he too had made all sorts of
resolutions about their relationship. If he had—a tiny
thrill ran through her at the thought—then the voyage
might be an even more memorable experience than
expected.

'And did you meet,' his voice had hardened to its
normal tones, 'Helen?' For a moment he paused and
when she did not answer he went on in the same edgy
voice, 'Helen Danielis?'

'No.' Jenni shook her head, wondering if he had
noticed that she was now wearing her hair loose, 'I
met a young man in the corridor. Michael he said his
name was.'

'Michaelis is Helen's brother. You will meet her at dinner. She has gone to lie down, I believe. It takes her some time to become used to the motion of the ship—although I would have thought it was smooth enough.'

'I think it's exhilarating.'

'And so do I.' It was the charmingly accented English of the young woman who with her husband had picked up Jenni and Dina at the flat, and Jenni turned to her with a mixture of relief and disappointment.

Sofia's amused glance rested for just an instant on Jenni's pink cheeks before she smiled at Perikles and slipped an affectionate arm into his. She was, thought Jenni, a perfect example of the wealthy sailing set, elegantly yet functionally dressed in navy Bermuda shorts with a pink and navy striped tee-shirt. On the top of her head, her blonde hair tucked firmly inside, she wore a yachting cap at a rakish angle. It was all calculated to foster the pretence that at some time she would give a hand with some of the chores, but looking at the beautifully manicured fingers Jenni doubted that they ever did anything more manual than dispensing coffee from a silver pot.

'Now,' Sofia ended a little homily with a dismissive tap on Perikles's arm, 'off you go and look after the ship, darling.' She spoke English well with an attractive raciness. 'Jenni and I want to talk.'

'All right.' His smile in Jenni's direction was indulgent and companionable. 'I think there's some tea being made, so I'll have some sent to you. See you later. *Andio.*'

'Now,' Sofia pulled two chairs into the shade of an awning and sat down on one, her rope-soled sandals reaching out for a comfortable position on one of the rails, 'come and sit down, Jenni.'

'Well,' Jenni wasn't too certain of what her position was to be on this voyage, 'I wonder if I should just run down and see how Dina is.'

'Of course not.' The other woman showed no uncertainty. 'I told Paul to keep them amused. I don't see why the children should always be the woman's job, do you?'

'Well, no. But I'm not married, and sometimes theories fall down when you try to put them into practice. Besides,' Jenni subsided on to the edge of the chair, 'I always thought that in Greek households it was the men who decided these things.'

'That is so,' Sofia agreed equably. 'At least, on the surface, but not in our household. Paul and I share these decisions. And luckily I produced a boy first time—a son is so important to Greek men. If Panos had been a girl then I would have had to keep on trying again until I had a child of the correct sex.' She wrinkled her short nose expressively. 'I shouldn't have cared for that at all. So there would have been friction.'

'I see.' Rather bemused, Jenni realised that she would have to adapt her views of how things were managed in Greek households. Sofia, for all her feminine exterior, gave the impression of a young woman who knew only too well what she wanted and how to get it. Just as Angela did. She couldn't imagine that Peri . . .

'Have you met Helen?' Sofia's sharp question interrupted Jenni's straying thoughts.

'Helen? No. Peri,' the name came to her lips shyly, a fact which she was certain wouldn't miss her companion's interested ears, 'told me that she'd gone to lie down. I believe she suffers from seasickness.'

'Oh.' Wrinkling her nose again, Sofia indicated a complete lack of sympathy.

'But I met her brother—Michaelis he said his name was.'

'Ah yes. And what did you think of him?'

'He seemed pleasant enough.' Jenni tried to remember what the young man whom she had met in the corridor looked like, but he had made so very little impression that she failed.

'Oh yes,' Sofia echoed her words disparagingly, 'he's pleasant enough.' She paused, looking at Jenni with a mischievous, almost wicked expression. 'I wonder if he'll achieve what he's set himself out to do.'

'And what is that?'

'Why, marry his sister off to Perikles, of course. Don't you know that's what half the unattached females in Greece have set their hearts on? And she might just succeed.'

Jenni felt a sudden jolt in the pit of her stomach. 'Is she very attractive?' She strove, successfully she thought, for an impassive expression.

'Oh, very.' Sofia paused. 'If you care for that style— I don't myself. But she does have an advantage that so many of her rivals lack.'

'And that is?' Jenni knew that she should have avoided the question, but somehow the words slipped from her lips.

'Oh, that her name is Danielis. You see,' she spoke slowly as if she knew that her words were tormenting to her listener, 'not only are her family owners of the famous airline, and that itself must be of great interest to Peri with so much of his fortune tied up in the hotel business, but also——' she paused for a long time while she rummaged in her linen bag for a pack of cigarettes which she offered to Jenni, who shook her head, then slowly she lit it and took a long deep breath. 'Also,' she began again, 'years ago Peri was madly in love with her aunt.'

'Her aunt?' Jenni was trying to work out this complicated relationship.

'Yes. You know these old Greek families. There were quite a number of children and Helen—she was Helen too—was the youngest. So you see, the combination, the airline and the name Helen Danielis, could quite easily prove irresistible to Peri.'

Jenni was grateful that the arrival of a tray with tea and biscuits intervened just as Sofia finished speaking so that there was no need for any reply to the information. She watched while the girl who had brought the tray pulled up a table and set it down close to Sofia's hand, then reached out to take the cup when it was offered.

'Is the girl a member of the crew?' she asked.

'The girl? Oh, the one who brought the tea?' Sofia spoke without interest. 'Yes. At least, her husband looks after the boat for Peri. The other two men just come aboard when she sails, but George and Maro are on board all the time. She cooks when we're on holiday. But,' there was a hint of pique in her voice now, 'you didn't ask about what happened to Peri and Helen, the other Helen.'

'No, I didn't.' Jenni had the feeling that she'd rather not know, but politeness forced the question to her lips. 'What did happen?'

'She was killed. One of their own aircraft crashed into a mountainside when she was flying to meet him in Berne. Peri was waiting at the airport when the news came through.' Sofia spoke with ghoulish relish.

'Oh.' Jenni felt the pain of it herself. 'How awful! No wonder he . . .' Abruptly she stopped, unwilling to admit to Sofia that she found him awkward.

'No wonder he what?' Sofia could hardly hide her curiosity.

'I don't know what I was going to say. Maybe that I got the impression he was a bit withdrawn.'

'Oh, he isn't that.' Sofia laughed as if the very idea was ridiculous. 'A bit reserved, maybe, but only with people he doesn't know.'

'And there's never,' even as she asked the question Jenni felt just a little bit ashamed of probing, 'been anyone else?'

'Oh, goodness, yes!' Again Sofia laughed. 'There have been dozens. I'm sure Peri has been no saint. But he's never shown any interest in marriage. At least,' she qualified significantly, 'not until now.'

Soon after that Jenni made the excuse that she ought to go and see to Dina and was able to escape. She couldn't explain why she should have been so reluctant to hear what Sofia had to tell her, especially when for the past week queries about Perikles Drimakos's private life had been very much in her thoughts. It wasn't as if she were naturally prim about gossip. Like most people she had a natural curiosity and enjoyed hearing about other people's lives. But on this occasion . . .

Below decks Jenni found Dina still happily engaged with Panos, who had graciously allowed her to help him with a jigsaw puzzle he had just started. Dina seemed prepared to accept with something like gratitude his remonstrations when she tried to force a piece into a wrong position, and his long-suffering sighs were received with contented smiles.

Neither of the two small heads bent so industriously over the table looked up when she went into the salon, and Paul who had been sitting with a book rose and walked to the door to speak to her.

'They're all right.' His English was more difficult to understand than his wife's. 'Soon they'll tire of this and want to do something else. I shall bring Dina along to the cabin when they finish.'

'Thank you.' Jenni spoke as softly as he did, grateful that now she had the opportunity to share with some other adults the responsibility of looking after the not very easy child. Then she went along the corridor until she came to the cabin which she and Dina were to share.

It was tiny but beautifully finished, with shining dark wood emphasising the feeling of luxury which had been achieved in such a small space. There were two bunk beds, one above the other, the upper of which Dina had immediately claimed for her own. Both had pink pillows and duvets in a slightly deeper shade and, Jenni had been relieved to find, thick comfortable mattresses.

Beneath the window was a small table which doubled as a desk and dressing table with the middle section opening up to reveal a mirror. On the wall opposite the bunks were two doors, the first concealing a wardrobe with sufficient hanging space and several useful shelves and the other opening into what Jenni considered the most luxurious of all, a tiny room with shower, toilet and washbasin.

When they had come aboard they had been met by a member of the crew, a short young man whose skin was burned almost black with sun and sea air and whose frequent smile was the more dazzling in consequence. Although she had been unable to understand the conversation there had been no escaping the look of satisfaction on Sofia's face when she was shown the cabin she was to occupy.

'Peri is a darling—really,' she assured Jenni and Paul and anyone else who could understand. 'Giving us the master suite. I should have thought that Helen . . . But you,' she turned her attention to her son, 'you, Panos, will have the small dressing-room. You will like that, won't you, being so close to Mama and Papa?'

Panos muttered something which suggested that he didn't find the prospect all that alluring, but by then Jenni was too intrigued by her brief glimpse of the master suite to pay much attention.

She could see a huge bed, raised on a kind of platform, its headboard padded with velvet in the same shade of dark red as the carpet. A cream silk material covered the bed and hung at the row of small high windows in the mahogany-lined walls. Before the door closed there was just time to notice two easy chairs covered in chintz and a large wooden chest with brass bindings, all combining in an air of restrained luxury. Doubtless the room had its own bathroom as well as the dressing-room Sofia had mentioned, making a fabulously comfortable apartment which the captain would normally occupy.

By the time Dina returned from her game with Panos, Jenni had showered and was lying on top of her bunk wearing nothing but a long blue kaftan a friend had brought her back from a holiday in Morocco and which she had decided to wear for dinner that night.

For once Dina didn't demand her attention but climbed the short wooden ladder to the upper berth and lay singing to herself and looking at a book which Panos had lent to her. After that there was silence for a while, disturbed only by the occasional rustle of paper and then just, silence.

It was idyllic when they went up on deck just before nine o'clock to find the boat anchored in a quiet bay a few hundred yards off the shore of a small island. Although the sky was dark as velvet the night seemed light, a contradiction which Jenni found explained when she looked up and saw the millions of stars scattered over the heavens. She could hear the soft lap of water against the hull, and still softer although just as beguiling was the sound of bozouki music coming from somewhere in the stern. Even Dina seemed to be affected by the strange magic of the night, for she slipped her hand into Jenni's as they hesitated in the doorway before anyone noticed their presence.

Paul and Panos were there and of course Sofia, looking sensational in a long clinging dress in an iridescent green material which was a perfect foil for her fair colouring. She had a proprietorial hand on her host's arm while she spoke with animation to Michaelis and the short dark girl who Jenni knew must be Helen. But before there was time to do more than notice, Perikles looked up immediately, catching her attention.

For what seemed to be a long time they stood looking at each other, Jenni forgetting everyone else there, forgetting even the small warm hand enclosed in hers. Till at last the tall figure came towards them, moving with that athletic easy stride which she had noticed the first time they had met. Tonight he was dressed comfortably in pale slacks and a white shirt with just a bit of formality in the paisley-pattern silk tie and the long sleeves fastened with filigree silver cufflinks.

'*Yassou.*' There was a dark caressing quality in his

voice which she had never heard before and which caused a curious tremor in the pit of her stomach. Without taking his eyes from hers, he bent down towards Dina, straightening up with the child in his arms while his lips curved into a faint half-mocking smile as if even he were amused, disconcerted by his actions.

Jenni knew that his first glance had taken in every detail of her appearance and she was filled with joy that her hair, fresh washed, was in loose waves falling to her shoulders, that the dark blue of her eyes was deepened, exaggerated with the liberal application of a shimmery violet shadow which she had bought in Piraeus that very morning. It had been hideously expensive, so that she had almost turned and run from the shop when the assistant had told her how much it cost. There had been a sudden flashing recollection of how very disapproving Jeremy would be if he could be a witness to such extravagance. But then firmly she had put that behind her, softening her feelings of guilt by the assurance that it wasn't every day that she had the chance of a holiday on a luxury yacht.

And now, the expression of Perikles Drimakos's face told her that every dinar had been well spent—on the eye-shadow, on the lip colour, on the mascara which made her already dark thick lashes feel positively heavy. At last she felt the spell which had kept her so long silent begin to ease.

'Hello.' Absurdly she felt shy.

'Come and have a drink.' Still carrying Dina, he led the way forward to where the others were waiting and as he began the introductions he took a glass from a tray and handed it to her.

'Michaelis you have met, of course, and this is his sister, Helen Danielis.' His voice softened as he spoke her name and Jenni wondered if it was for this girl or for the other one long dead whom he had loved so madly.

She would not have thought this Helen would have attracted his attention to the point of marriage. She was small and dark, doll-like, and her fingers resting so briefly in Jenni's felt delicate and brittle like a bird's. Her eyes were her most striking feature, large and luminous, seeming almost to swallow the whole of her face.

She was dressed in pink, in a style that was much too old for her, and her fine dark hair was drawn severely back from her rather sharp features and twisted into a knot at the back of her head. She could scarcely be more than eighteen or nineteen, Jenni decided, then she remembered with a pang that many mature men had a distinct preference for very young girls. That was especially true of very rich men, you had to look no farther than the gossip columns to confirm that. She stole a hasty glance at Perikles and saw that indeed he was looking at Helen, but his expression revealed nothing of his feelings. At that same moment he bent so that Dina could slip from his arms and run to join Panos.

During the meal, which was served under an awning at one side of the deck, the conversation was general and there was a good deal of laughter. Jenni found herself sitting between Paul and Michaelis, both of whom seemed determined to vie with each other in a lighthearted attempt to gain her favour, a situation which she found both stimulating and enjoyable. Once or twice she looked up to the top of the table where Perikles sat between Helen and Sofia, each time gaining the impression that he was more interested in the conversation down at the end of the table than in what his partners were saying. A good deal of wine was being consumed, although Jenni, with a recollection of what had happened the previous night, chose deliberately to curtail the amount she drank.

They had a delicious meal which was served by George and Maro, who joined in the general merriment, totally uninhibited, it appeared, in their relationship with their employer. Although she could not understand what was being said it was a novel experience for Jenni to watch the changing expressions of pleasure which chased over his face. She had thought her scrutiny unobserved until quite suddenly she became aware that she in turn was being as carefully studied. Her hand shook as she hastily reached out for her glass, her eyes moved quickly away.

Much later, when she had said goodnight to all the others and having put Dina into her bunk and waited till she fell soundly asleep, Jenni quietly closed the door of her cabin and walked quickly up to the now silent deck. It was strange that the others had felt so tired—or rather, it was strange that she didn't. Strange, because the sea air was generally believed to have that effect on people. And yet tonight, this one night, she felt gloriously, vitally alive.

Jenni sighed as she leaned negligently against the rail and looked dreamily towards the dark shape of the island just ahead of them. She breathed deeply, filling her lungs with that evocative scent of thyme and lemon balm which permeated the atmosphere. Then a different scent caught at her nostrils, a faint whiff of something that brought her heart hammering into her throat. No power on earth could have stopped her turning round to search for the faint glow that would locate him. And even as she did so, he came forward to her, out of the shadows, tossing the scarcely smoked cigar away from them in a shining arc.

'I . . . I didn't see you.' The tumult of her pulses almost stopped the words in her throat and she was surprised to hear her own voice.

'No?' In the dark the strange slanting eyes glittered with the brilliance of jet. He said nothing more but continued to look at her till in sheer self-defence she forced herself to turn away.

'It's such a beautiful night.'

He ignored the banal remark and his next words startled her. 'What were you thinking of,' his head jerked towards the table where they had eaten, 'there?'

'I don't know.' Desperately she pressed her hands together, her eyes were rigidly fixed on the horizon. 'All sorts of things.' She tried to laugh.

'Jenni.' Her body melted as he spoke her name for the first, the very first time. His hand came out towards her, sliding beneath the thick silky fall of her hair and circling her slender neck. 'Jenni.' With forceful gentleness he turned her towards him. 'You were wondering about something earlier tonight. I want to know what it was. Tell me.'

'I was thinking,' it was pleasure for her to give up all the resistance to him, to raise her hands and put cool fingers to the corners of his eyes, 'I was thinking that there's something else in you, not just Greek blood.'

His grin was sudden, flashing white, reminding her at once of half-forgotten tales of long-dead heroes. 'What do you think I am?' His voice was low, almost a whisper, bringing all kinds of sensations tingling along her spine.

She shook her head, laughing with sudden joy while at the same time her fingers slid slowly from his cheeks, resting on his shoulders. 'I don't know.'

'Nor I.' The wide shoulders shrugged, rippling beneath her fingers. 'In the past my family were seafarers and there is a story that a ten-times-great-grandmother was a Manchurian princess taken by force by my forebear. But you know that we Greeks are great ones for legend.'

'You don't believe it?'

'Oh yes, I believe it all right. But only in the same way that I believe all the old stories about Aphrodite, and the Minotaur. And Androcles,' he added after a brief pause.

'Oh.' Jenni felt the warmth in her cheeks, but this time was able to laugh at herself. 'Oh, him.' Suddenly aware of what she was doing, she let her hands slip from his shoulders.

'But why are you walking out on deck at this time of night? You ought to be in bed.' He took his hands away from her neck and leaned against the rail of the yacht, his head still turned towards her, studying the profile she averted from him.

'I didn't feel like sleeping. And you know, nights like this are meant to be savoured. I suppose they're commonplace to you, but to us in England . . .'

'Ah yes, you in England.' Then with a sudden change of direction, 'When are you to be married, Miss Cotterell?'

The sudden formality struck her like a blow so that she could hardly remember the question he had asked.

'Married?' she asked stupidly.

'Yes, when are you and Jeremy,' he paused, 'when are you to become Jenni and Jeremy?' Again his voice assumed that particularly condescending tone which she disliked so much, which made the two names sound so ridiculous together.

'It hasn't been decided yet.' That was true enough, for Jeremy had been extremely vague on the subject. 'And I don't know why you're so determined to make it sound amusing.' Her hurt brought an edge to her voice and her mind raced in an attempt to find some way of hitting back. 'Jenni and Jeremy are no more humorous than Jenni and . . . and Perikles would be.'

She turned to face him her eyes sparkling in sudden anger, but when she saw the expression in his eyes she knew what he was thinking. 'And,' she rushed on before she had time to consider more carefully what she ought to say, 'I'm sorry if that offends your ego, Mr Drimakos. I know that most girls would be very pleased to combine their names with yours, but I'm not one of them.'

'I don't know why you're working yourself into such a state about it, Miss Cotterell. Even the most innocent conversation with you seems to end in a slanging match!'

Jenni tried taking several long slow breaths, but before she could stop them her impetuous indignation burst out again. 'You're perhaps so used to sycophants about you, Mr Drimakos, that you don't realise just how you do speak to other people. That's why you dislike almost everything I say.'

'I didn't know that I did.' The sweet reason in his tone was most irritating.

'That's what I was saying. You're so used to women agreeing with you you can't understand it when they don't. Most of them are only too delighted to be noticed by the great Perikles Drimakos.' Jenni was really warming to her theme and spoke her next words with such conviction that she almost fooled herself. 'But I'm not one of them, I'm afraid. I'm sorry, and I don't mean to be rude.' She smiled as if she had the slightest intention of softening her words. 'Perhaps it's because I'm unlike those other women that I'm not in the least bit in awe of you—or your money.' If she had been less anxious in her disclaimer she might have noticed the way his lips tightened at the corners, but she plunged on in case what she had said still left him with doubts. 'As a man you mean nothing to me, Mr Drimakos.'

They stared at each other and she had time now to see the blaze of anger in his eyes, the mouth a straight hard gash. A faint shiver ran through her as she heard her foolish words echoing in her mind. It was a long time before he spoke and to her surprise his tones were calm and even, giving no hint of the anger she had seen flash on his features.

'Don't challenge me, Miss Cotterell. A challenge is something I find very difficult to resist.'

'I hadn't intended it as a challenge,' she answered coldly.

'Whether you intended it or not,' even his expression had become mild now and his voice was deep, soft as silk, 'and in case you're under any misapprehension, just remember this, Miss Cotterell. The situation between us is exactly how *I* intend it to be. Your wishes on the matter simply have no importance. I decide how things will be in my own life and I allow no one the opportunity to call the tune. Do you really think,' and now there was an edge of laughter in his voice, an edge which made Jenni feel callow and ridiculous, 'do you really think that if I cared enough I couldn't have you eating out of my hand?'

The eyes blazed wickedly in the dark face and she heard a sound of amusement deep, deep down in his chest. 'I have the feeling that if I were to do that,' the suddenness with which he raised a hand and snapped his fingers made her jump, but his eyes still held hers mesmerically, 'we would find that your reactions would be the same as every other woman I've ever met. You would have no power in the matter. So before you issue any challenge,' his voice dropped even lower and he took a step towards her, 'or say anything that could be construed as a challenge, think of that, Jenni.' While he paused she could feel something sensuous trembling at the base of her spine. 'If I wanted to do so, I could soon change your will to coincide with my own.' His teeth flashed suddenly in the darkness, seeming to lighten the fraught intensity of the exchange. 'But only—only, Miss Cotterell—if I wished it to be so.'

For a long time they stood staring at each other and gradually Jenni felt the slowing, the relaxing of her impetuous pulses, and at the same time she had the impression that his amusement had been fleeting, that now he was as disturbed as she was herself. And her own agitation was impossible to deny. Her heart was clamouring inside her body, her hands were clammy with sweat, the palms pierced with the pressure of her fingernails. As she looked into those glittering dark eyes a ripple of something very much like fear ran down her spine.

Then he spoke with such weariness that she longed to put her head on his breast and weep, like a child longing for comfort.

'Go to bed, Jenni. It was a mistake for you to come up on deck so late. And if I offended you then I apologise. I'm sure that Jeremy is a very worthy young man.' He sighed faintly and turned abruptly from her. 'I promised Merope that you would enjoy this holiday, so let us forget what has happened, shall we?'

'Of course.' She ignored his cruel reminder of the

reason for her being on this trip in the first place. 'After all, we aren't children, are we?'

'No.' His face was all dark planes, tense and forbidding.

'Then I'll say goodnight.' Without waiting for an answer she whirled away from him, glad when she reached her cabin and the opportunity of letting the tears course silently down her cheeks.

CHAPTER FIVE

WHEN she woke in the morning it seemed to Jenni that she had been asleep for only a few minutes, and she lay looking out through the small window at the patch of blue sky. That was how she always felt when she had drunk more than one glass of wine, she reminded herself. And of course the fact that she had lain for hours crying hadn't helped. She touched her eyelids, wondering if they looked as swollen as they felt.

Gently, unwilling to disturb Dina before she woke naturally, she eased herself out of the narrow bed and went to the bathroom. Dispassionately she surveyed herself in the mirror while she filled a glass with water which she drank at one long draught. She didn't look as bad as she had thought, not half as bad as she felt. True, her eyelids were a bit red and swollen and her face beneath the suntan was pale, but it was nothing that anyone else would notice. And by the time she had a cold shower ... Shivering slightly, she threw aside her cotton nightie and stepped under the gush of cool water.

Last night over dinner it had been decided that they would spend the morning swimming and skin-diving and that in the afternoon heat they would sail farther along towards Paros. So when they appeared on deck Jenni and Dina were wearing their swimsuits, each with a blouse on top, Dina with a large straw hat to protect her from the fierceness of the sun, while Jenni made do with a scarf tied gypsy fashion round her head.

She felt a bit shy as she went on deck, wishing that the next few hours were over, but when she joined the crowd round the table Perikles Drimakos's greeting gave no indication that anything untoward had happened between them after the others had gone to bed last night. In fact his query towards her and his niece was banal in its ordinariness.

'Did you sleep well, Jenni?' Both pairs of eyes were concealed behind tinted glass, but still she felt that his would be much more perceptive than any of the others', would see through the lie even before she spoke it—and would undoubtedly be amused by her reason.

'Very well.' Blandly she returned his gaze before turning to Dina. 'We both did.'

As they sat down to join in the meal of ripe melon followed by freshly baked rolls with chilled butter and strong delicious coffee, Jenni allowed the chatter of the others to wash over her. The discussion was on the relative merits of swimming from the boat or from the shore, so she was unable to add anything. But once or twice she caught Perikles's eyes on her, searching with an intensity that brought colour to her face, a tormenting throbbing to her pulses. With an attempt at coolness she turned deliberately away from him, feigning an interest in how the others were dressed.

All the men were wearing trunks topped by casual shirts and Paul had a cotton trilby perched on the back of his head. Sofia had on a black bikini of exaggerated brevity which the see-through cover-up did nothing to make more modest, while Helen was wearing a pink towelling robe over her swimming gear.

Because Helen insisted that she didn't really want to swim and with the children to consider as well, it was decided to take the dinghy to the beach and use that as a base. When they reached the shore, they found plenty of shade in the fringe of olive trees tilting over the wide swathe of pale soft sand and soon spread out mats where they could lie in comfort.

'I'm going to rest for a while.' Sofia began to rub her arms and legs with sun oil, then turned her attention to the pile of paperback books she had brought with her. Helen sat and watched the preparations the men were making for scuba-diving before lying down with a sigh and closing her eyes.

'I'll watch Dina, Jenni,' Sofia offered amiably. 'To tell the truth I'm not all that keen on the water. I'd much rather lie here in the shade. And the kids look as if they're happy enough.' As she pushed her sunglasses up on her nose she looked over towards where Panos and Dina were happily engaged in building some sort of castle while they chattered incomprehensibly.

'You're sure?' Jenni looked uncertainly towards where Helen was lying, still dressed in her towelling robe, eyes firmly closed. Sofia too looked at the recumbent figure and wrinkled her nose expressively.

'Sure.' Sofia grinned and lay back, adjusting the small pillow at her neck, wriggling to make comfortable hollows for her hips. 'You can do the same for me some time.' She yawned as if she too had had a restless night and closed her eyes.

Keeping her eyes firmly averted from the group of men and from the tallest of them in particular, Jenni went over to where the children were playing and bent down to speak, but as her enquiries were met only by brief abstracted replies she decided that it was safe enough to leave them.

She ran down to the water's edge, masochistically enjoying the sensation of sand burning the soles of her feet, but grateful when she reached the damp area where the water lapped against the shore. Only then did she discard the blouse she had been wearing, throwing it with a careless hand on to the high dry sand behind her, stretching with sudden joy as the blissful warmth of the sunshine caressed her skin.

When she walked into the water, feeling the warm coolness of it creep up her legs, over her thighs, when she tipped forward so that her body broke the surface, she exulted in all the sensations. Easily she swam through the calm aquamarine sea, aware of the salty clean tang of it on her lips, of her sodden hair floating behind her like seaweed.

After a bit she rested, lying face down on the surface, all the disturbances of the night washed away in the pleasure she felt as she watched the soft colours of the pebbles on the sea-bed catching and reflecting the sun's rays. Among them sea anemones waved delicately, tempting the tiny silvery fish swimming above them to come near. Her hands flipped, pushing herself effortlessly along till with a sudden decision she dived steeply down, picked up a large pink shell, and shot to the surface again, almost colliding with another swimmer.

'Sorry,' she gasped, knowing even before she had shaken the water from her eyes who had pursued her.

'My fault,' he said with a hint of stiffness before he smiled, making her heart miss a beat, then race frantically as she saw him throw his head back to get rid of the hair which had washed down on to his face. Drops of crystal clung to his long dark lashes while the dark eyes looked sardonically.

'Look!' Breathlessly Jenni held out the shell, her entranced eyes going from his to the pearl pink of the inner surface. 'I got this for Dina.'

As they both trod water, Perikles put out a hand to take it from her and she imagined that his fingers lingered on hers for longer than was strictly necessary.

'Mmm.' Her face seemed to demand more attention than the gift for his niece. 'How did you get such eyes, Jenni? Did you know that they're the colour of the ocean?'

Her senses bounded in wild pleasure. 'Perhaps my forebears were seafarers too.'

He laughed, and in a mood of rare amiability they turned towards the shore and began slowly to crawl towards it. 'You're a good swimmer—I suppose you know that.'

The unimportant little compliment made her feel accomplished and significant. 'I used to swim for my county.' She paused. 'And last year Jeremy and I went diving in Cornwall.'

'Jeremy again.' This time the only mockery was for himself. He spoke as if Jeremy's existence was an obstacle to his plans, and Jenni was happy to join in the laughter.

'I came to ask if you'd like to go out to the rocks and do some diving. We can go only two at a time. Michaelis and Paul are setting off now.'

'I'd love to.' She was breathless again at the implication that they would go together.

'Good.' They reached the shallows and together walked towards where she had left her blouse. As she pulled it about her shoulders, selfconsciously aware of Perikles' intense gaze, she was suddenly glad that she had a good figure. She wasn't as petite as Sofia nor as painfully thin as Helen, but she was slender enough, with a narrow waist and curves just in the right places. And her legs were all right. In fact when she had pulled on the plain black swimsuit back in the cabin she had been quite pleased with its effect. It was a stretchy black crêpe material cut straight across above the bust and with one strap whose ends met in the centre front. It did, she thought, give just as clear an idea of her shape as Sofia's infinitely more revealing bikini. And it was much more tantalising. She caught sight of the expression on Perikles' face and turned away with heightened colour.

'Your shell.' His low-pitched drawl stopped her and she held out her hand without looking back. But when their fingers touched again there was no mistaking the warning messages her senses were sending to her brain. She ran over the sand towards the children—away, away from him.

Their diving expedition was like an excursion into another world. Jenni was grateful for the knowledge she had picked up the previous year that enabled her to understand the equipment, but apart from that there was little similarity between that adventure and this.

It was the water, of course, that was the main difference. This warm, brilliantly clear element was unlike any ever found off the coast of Britain. But besides that there was something so tranquil about being with Perikles, being guided by his confident expert hand as they swam together down into caverns under the rocks. Behind the face mask she smiled her appreciation as he pointed to some crabs scuttling among the stones and to a particularly beautiful mass of seaweed which drifted hypnotically in the current.

Once or twice they surfaced while he checked that she wasn't feeling too tired, but always she insisted on going under again, following his dark powerful body as it flipped down towards the sea-bed. Even then Jenni was wondering which she found most fascinating, the shoals of tiny shimmering fish that appeared undisturbed by the strangers, or the man who was making this journey possible. Her mind veered away from a direct answer to her question.

At last she decided it was time to go back, as much because she was worried about leaving Dina for too long as because of fatigue.

'In any case we'll be able to do this again.' He pulled the short rope which started the engine of the dinghy. 'You should see as much as you can while you're here.'

'Yes.' Jenni averted her mind firmly from this reminder that soon she would be returning to England. 'Thank you for taking me.'

'I enjoyed it.' He leaned back, one hand steadying the tiller as they began to move round the headland towards the beach. 'It isn't often I get the opportunity to show off the natural fauna and flora to an intelligent visitor.' Then as if regretting that he had said so much he turned so that she was presented with a view of his back, as dark and uncompromising as ever.

They had a picnic lunch on the beach, all spread out and ready by the time Perikles and Jenni returned, with the children impatient to begin eating. First they ate chilled consommé, spicy and refreshing, then hunks of bread eaten with feta cheese washed down with wine for those who wanted it, fruit juice for the others. Both Perikles and Jenni were with the children in the latter group, and she thought there was nothing quite so delicious when you were thirsty as cold freshly squeezed orange.

'Uncle Peri.' When they had finished eating and were lying drowsily in the shade Dina went up and laid her head against his bare chest.

'Yes?'

'What shall we do now?' There was a hint of the old whingeing note in her voice.

'I just want to rest.' Jenni, who was watching, saw

his hand move idly over the child's dark hair, and it brought a curious yearning feeling to her chest. 'I'm sleepy.'

'Yes. But what can *I* do?' There was no doubt whom she considered the most important.

'Come with me, Dina.' Jenni forced herself to her feet and crossed the few feet of sand, skirting the others in the group who had given in to the siesta habit. 'And I'll tell you a story.'

Dina was about to struggle from his grasp when suddenly it tightened. 'No—no.' Although soft his voice was firm. 'Your aunt is tired too. Sit down, Jenni.' The eyelids that had been closed opened lazily and he was watching her with an expression that seemed to belie his claim to fatigue. 'Come on.' He moved slightly so that there was room for her beside him on the wide straw mat. 'We can sleep together.' As his eyes closed his lips curved into a faint smile. 'All three of us.'

'Come on, Auntie Jen,' speaking as softly as her uncle so that none of the others could hear, 'let's all sleep together.'

Jenni lay down, her heart thudding with the emotion that sooner or later she was going to have to name. Pulling the sunglasses down from the top of her head, she lay back, looking at the pattern of gnarled branches, grey leaves and blue sky. Beside her Dina adjusted to a more comfortable position between them and to help her Peri eased his grip. And his hand relaxed against Jenni's bare arm.

Numb with longing, she stifled the moaning little sigh that rose to her lips, wondering if he too was conscious of this strange chemical reaction between them. They had only to speak to each other and they quarrelled, she hurling insults in a way that would have shocked any of her friends who could have overheard. And yet all the time her body was aware of him, almost indecently aware.

Determinedly she closed her eyes, trying to shut out any chance sight of that dark form lying so close. But at once, as if the image were projected on to the inner surface of her eyelids, she saw him as he had been just before lunch, swinging first Panos, then Dina round in wide circles, then dropping them shrieking on to the sand.

She had been watching. Secretly with an almost unwilling compulsion while she made a pretence of squeezing the sea water from her dripping hair. The shoulders were as broad as they had appeared under the fine suiting which usually covered them, the brown chest was sprinkled with hair, black, glossy, curling. When he looked up suddenly and caught her eyes on him she turned, with as much carelessness as she could muster, so that her flaming cheeks would be hidden from him.

But now, lying so close to him, his fingers resting so casually against her arm, where there was no one watching her, she could relax, give herself up to the trembling pleasure of the contact. But even as she did so, the child stirred sleepily and Perikles' fingers moved, leaving her. Jenni's sigh was so light that no one heard, and she lay still, listening to the tumult of her heartbeats grow more restrained, return to a state more like normality. That was a great relief, she told herself as she drifted off into a brief sleep.

Every experience since her arrival in Greece seemed larger than life, and this stopping off spot in Paros was no exception, Jenni decided. They had been sailing and swimming, diving and sleeping their way through the islands, and Peri had promised the children that when they reached Paroikia, the main town, they would go to a picture show. Unable to decide whether or not to believe him, nevertheless Jenni had been fascinated by the lighthearted man who seemed in such direct contrast to the cold forbidding stranger whom she had first met. More and more often it seemed that his eyes had turned to her for confirmation of a new tolerant relationship developing between them.

Like last night, for instance, when they had met on deck after the others had gone to bed. It was becoming almost a ritual, one that they both looked forward to as an antidote to the perfection of their days of happy lazing. Even so, much of the sharpness had gone from their exchanges. There was not the same desire to score and wound as there had been, it was more a gentle tolerant teasing, infinitely preferable, something which one of his first remarks told her he had noticed too.

'Merope would be very pleased if she could see us now.'

'Would she?' Jenni stood with her face looking forward, pleasantly conscious of his eyes on her profile. She considered carefully before she answered. 'I think I must revise my opinion of the Greek male.'

'Oh?' He was cagily curious.

'Yes. You see,' her tone was bland and innocent, 'I had this idea of a patriarchal society, one where the male was paramount, and yet on every side I see henpecked men.'

'Are you putting me into that category?' Again, self-control was the keynote.

'I was thinking in particular of Angie and Giannis, Sofia and Paul.' Her tongue was firmly in her cheek. 'But since you bring it up, perhaps there is something in your suggestion.' Her quick darting glance was deliberately provoking. 'You seem to be very concerned about your sister's good opinion.'

'You consider that a bad thing?' Still he was mild, amused.

'Of course not. I'm all in favour. I'm simply saying that I thought that in Greece it would be otherwise.'

'Did you, Miss Cotterell?' Suddenly his hands were on her shoulders, turning her fiercely towards him. 'Did you really? And can you tell me exactly how things are in England, can you deny that there too men like to be men?' The dark eyes blazed down at her in the darkness. Alien, exciting. 'Can you pretend to me that you are the dominant partner in your relationship with Jeremy?' He successfully avoided using the old scoffing note when he spoke the name.

'I . . . I don't know what you mean.' She despised her own uncertainty. 'Of course we decide everything together.'

'Come now, Jenni.' His voice softened with the use of her first name. 'You've told me that because of him you've tried all kinds of way-out ideas—all this simple living during the holidays, playing at being vegetarians. Can you tell me that you preferred that kind of existence to this?'

'Of course not.' Jenni regretted giving him so much material with which to attack her. 'But we're not all as rich as you are. We have to cut our clothes according to our cloth,' she finished primly.

At that he laughed with a hint of the old sarcasm. 'Well, I hope you aren't trying to make me feel guilty about being rich, because you'll never succeed. I don't mind being rich, not in the least. In fact I even enjoy it—much more, I imagine, than you and Jeremy will enjoy your hill farm in Wales. And what is more, because I'm rich I *can* help others to solve their problems.' Although he didn't say so she knew that he was making an oblique reference to Jeremy's job. Strangely that no longer offended. 'I employ a large number of people who through their work can enjoy things that a decade ago were outside their aspirations. *I've* enjoyed seeing them become more prosperous.'

'I don't doubt it.' She couldn't quite keep a note of coldness from her voice. 'But all I was saying was that . . .'

'Yes, I remember what you were saying, and,' his fingers tightened so that she felt the strength of them biting into her skin, 'let me assure you that when I marry I shall not allow my wife to dominate me. So don't,' his voice had become very low with an underlying note of menace, increasing the emotions trickling sensuously down her spine, 'let that idea run away with you, Miss Cotterell.'

But that had been last night, and a moment later they had been talking, laughing over something that had happened earlier in the day, the interlude of tension between them over as swiftly as it had come.

And now, sitting in the outdoor cinema, looking towards the screen where a posse of Western lawmen were chasing a group of bank robbers over impossible inhospitable country, Jenni decided that the film was a diversion she could well do without. It was such an incongruity in this setting. Overhead the sky fairly shimmered with stars and only yards away, when the sound of gunfire eased she could hear the lapping of water against one of the most perfect shorelines that could be imagined. She cast a glance at the others who made up the party, deciding that she was alone in her opinion, for the children were happily licking the choc-ices which were constantly available from a salesgirl, Sofia was drinking Coke through a straw and the others

were absorbed by the film. Peri she could not quite
see, as he was at the opposite end of the row from her
chair. She murmured a word to Helen who was beside
her and made her escape, moving quietly so that no
one else would be disturbed.

As she walked across the dunes to the shore she
pondered just a little about Helen, the girl who seemed
so remote, so utterly unlike the woman who would one
day marry Perikles Drimakos. And she remembered
the fraught little conversation she had overheard between Helen and her brother the other day. She and
Dina had been lying on their bunks quietly reading
with the door propped open an inch to increase the
cooling draught through the cabin.

At first Jenni had paid little attention to the low
conversation, although it was impossible to be un-
conscious of the passion in the voices even in a foreign
tongue. She had recognised who was speaking, but only
when the sound of a door closing had brought the conversation to a halt had she been offered any clue as to
the subject of their discussion.

'That Helen . . .' it was Dina's voice, dismissive,
absurdly adult and abstracted as she struggled with the
book Panos had given her. '. . . says she doesn't want
to marry Uncle Peri.'

Jenni felt her heart beating with accelerated interest,
but she was slow in answering. 'Doesn't she?'

'No.'

There was a long pause while Jenni wrestled with
her conscience, and lost. 'I wonder why.'

'I don't know. That's what Michaelis asked her.'

'And what did she say.'

'She said—you know that Michaelis. She was angry
with him, I think.'

Jenni listened for a long time to the sound of pages

being turned but dared not ask any further questions. She had given up hope of hearing any more when Dina spoke again. 'Anyway, I don't think Uncle Peri will want to marry her.'

'Why?' Lack of interest positively dripped from her voice.

'Oh, I don't know.' Dina closed her book with an expressive thud. 'If she married Uncle Peri would she be my auntie?'

'Mmm. Yes.'

'I don't want her to be my auntie, then.' A pair of brown legs dangled over the side of the bunk. 'I like Uncle Peri.'

'Oh?' Jenni prepared to receive the descending body. 'I thought you didn't.'

'Oh, that.' Dina didn't need to be reminded of the day of Jenni's arrival. 'I didn't like him that day. But most days I do.' Successfully she negotiated the descent, relaxing with a sigh against Jenni's comforting shoulder. 'But if he married Helen I wouldn't. Shall I tell him?'

'Oh, I shouldn't,' Jenni spoke hastily. 'Grown-ups don't always like to be told things like that. Best wait and see. Perhaps he doesn't mean to marry Helen at all.'

And that, she thought as she walked along the sand, was very much the impression she had. In spite of Sofia's whispers and knowing looks which could be very trying. There was nothing in Perikles' manner towards Helen that singled her out from anyone else. In fact he responded more to Sofia's flirtatious ways than to anything Helen might choose to say to him. And even if as Sofia suggested it was a marriage of families more than of two people it was strange that he showed no great sign of even modest affection.

No, she decided, kicking off her sandals and leaving them beside an outcrop of rock where she would be sure to find them later, the chances were that the marriage was a figment of Sofia's romantic, rather facile imagination. Jenni felt her spirits suddenly soar.

On the other hand, there was a possibility that this was how arranged marriages were organised—a matter-of-fact meeting between the parties, with a close relative as chaperone, so that they could get to know one another. Then the engagement would be announced. As she walked along a tiny outcrop of smooth rock that jutted out above a pool of clear still water her heart fell like a stone, up and down, as mercurial as some of the sillier girls in the Upper Fifth, she thought with a tiny stab of sympathy.

She stood for a moment above the water enjoying the soft kiss of a warm breeze against her skin, then with a totally unexpected decision she made up her mind that she would go for a swim. Her hair would get wet, but what did that matter, and in any case in this warm atmosphere it would dry quickly enough.

She was wearing the cream dress, the one that Jeremy had forbidden, and it was the work of a second to pull at the shoulder straps and step out of it, leaving it in a discarded bundle on the shore. A moment later she stepped forward, shivering slightly as much at her own daring as at the coolness of the water, then she struck out in a powerful crawl.

The feeling of freedom was heady, unimaginably adventurous and liberating as the water caressed her half-naked flesh. Several times she crossed the calm lagoon, as if the honour of Berkshire depended on her, then, all her fierce energy dispersed, she moved to the shore with a languid graceful stroke. When her hand touched the shore she threw back her head, relieved that her piled-up hair was less wet than she might have expected. One searching toe found a foothold and she was about to heave herself from the water when above her something moved, the dark shape of a man was clearly outlined against the velvet sky.

'Can I give you a hand?' Although she had instantly recognised him she was relieved to hear his voice so calm and even.

'No, thank you.' She sank back into the water, her hands held protectively against her bare breast. 'I can manage.'

'Come on, then.' The flash of white told her that she was the source of some amusement.

'I can't, of course,' it was the return of the cold war, 'until you turn round.'

'Come on, Miss Cotterell,' the old taunting note was back in his voice, 'as you said, we aren't children. I *have* seen naked women before.'

'I'm sure you have, Mr Drimakos. But as I told you before, I'm not one of them.'

'Do you intend to spend the night in the water, then?'

'If you intend to stand the night where you are I'll have no choice, shall I?'

'Oh, I don't know. Perhaps we could come to some compromise.'

'Such as?' With an effort she stopped her teeth from chattering.

'Such as . . .' As he drawled he reached into the pocket of his shirt took out one of his black cheroots and slowly lit it. 'Such as, I give you my handkerchief which will help to dry you, then you put your dress on and I'll wait for you. We can walk back to the cinema together, just in time to see the last reel.'

'Oh yes?' Jenni tried to find the snag in his tempting offer.

'No strings, Miss Cotterell.' He raised both arms and then let them drop. 'You needn't look so suspicious. Look.' He pulled a large folded handkerchief from his pocket and holding it by one corner dangled it in front of her eyes. 'Shall I leave it on top of your dress?' He paused and she imagined the dark eyes gleaming maliciously.' 'Ah, and by the way, Miss Cotterell, I like this dress. Much more than most of the others you wear. Is this one you chose for your fiancé?'

'No.' She spoke through gritted teeth. 'As a matter of fact Jeremy doesn't like it.' Put that in your pipe and smoke it! she thought.

'Doesn't he?' The mocking sympathy was extremely trying. 'Well, I always thought we'd have very different tastes.' He dropped the handkerchief on to the ground where she could see the white outline of her dress. 'I'll wait for you down here.' He jumped down on to the beach at the other side of the tiny spit of land, leaving her to clamber from the water in privacy.

As she dried herself with the totally inadequate scrap of cotton Jenni wondered why she had been such a complete idiot. It was totally out of character for her to do anything so foolish—to come for a stroll along the shore was one thing, to jump half-naked into the sea was quite another. And now to be once again at his mercy. To be obliged to borrow his handkerchief and no doubt to have to hear his remonstrations all the way back to the village.

She fumbled with her shoulder straps as she wriggled her damp body into the dress, irritated that the material should be so sticky, that it should cling so awkwardly. Then she jumped down to join Perikles where he stood on the fringe of the shore, staring out to sea, the glowing end of the cigar moving towards his mouth and away again.

He turned round when he heard her and she knew when she saw his face that his jocularity had been a mere façade, now his eyes raked her with angry aggression.

'Don't you think it was a bit stupid to come along here on your own with no one knowing where you were?'

'No.' She decided the only thing was to brazen it out so her reply was flip. 'Besides, I told Helen.'

'You can see what kind of people we get at these places nowadays. Women, even liberated women, can't always cope with the results of their own actions.'

'But nothing happened,' she persisted with the casual, mildly amused voice that she knew would be bound to irritate him. 'In any event, I can take care of myself.'

There was a long pause when she held her breath. She didn't like the way he was looking at her, but when he spoke his voice was so mild that she relaxed.

'Have you had any experience of that, Jenni?'

'What?' All kinds of sensations were rippling through her body as she tried to think what he had said. 'Do you mean have I had to look after myself?'

'Yes.' She watched while he ground out the butt of his cigar in the damp sand at his feet. 'That's what I mean. Have you ever had to fight off a man who, let's put it delicately,' his brief laugh caused a shiver to race down her spine, 'has one thing on his mind?'

'No,' she spoke boldly, 'but I think I could cope.' To her annoyance one of the bows she had tied in her shoulder strap loosened and began to slip down her shoulder.

'Let me.' Perikles spoke gently as his fingers reached

for the ends, tying them firmly while the touch of his skin against hers seemed to scorch the blood in her veins.

Then unexpectedly his hands tightened about her, pulling her round to face him. The next moment she had been thrown back against the sand and the whole weight of his body was lying against hers. Eyes wide with shock, she stared up at him, knowing that she was powerless, half fearful of what came next.

'And now what would you do, Jenni?' Each of her hands was caught in one of his, extended along the sand, his weight bearing down on her. 'Tell me,' he insisted mockingly.

Jenni tried to move her hands, but his were inflexible. 'I should scream.' She tried to speak easily. 'There are bound to be people who would hear.'

'But they are all engrossed in the shoot-out—listen.' For a moment they lay there, hearing the whine of bullets from the direction of the village. 'And anyone else would be bound to ignore any shouts. It's surprising how often such things are heard along this coast. And shouting,' he spoke with detachment, 'in the situation you are now in wouldn't necessarily be the best course. All it needs is this . . .'

His mouth closing over hers was so unexpected, so blissfully unexpected that her whole body relaxed, melted for the instant that it lasted. Then he had withdrawn and was looking down at her with an angry expression. 'So you see just how easy it would be.'

'Yes,' Jenni felt as if her heart was breaking, 'I do see. I'm sorry.'

Perikles rolled away from her and was extending a hand to help her to her feet. She had a moment to notice the beads of moisture on his forehead before he grinned at her. 'You know, Miss Cotterell, that's something I never expected to hear you say.' He touched her cheek with a gentle, tender finger. 'You forgive me for such a forceful lesson, *agape mou*?'

'Yes.' It was a whisper and her heart was soaring with sudden joy. To hear an endearment on his lips seemed all the pleasure that life could hold.

CHAPTER SIX

SHE was in love with him—there was no point in concealing that fact from herself any longer. And it had existed from almost that first moment when she saw him in his office in the centre of Athens. Although she hadn't recognised it she had been fighting an attraction, something irresistible, something totally outside her experience.

But now she lay back against the closed door of her cabin, not even troubling to look towards the upper berth so she could check that Dina was asleep. Now she rubbed her hands over her arms; it was bliss to give herself to the acknowledgement of what she was feeling, to allow the dreamy pleasure of what had happened to wash over her. And even the realisation that Perikles showed no sign of returning her feelings seemed not to matter. Just then it was enough to know that he disliked her less than he had way back in the early days of their acquaintance, nearly two weeks ago.

For two days more they drifted about the islands, stopping where the fancy took them at tiny uninhabited islands whose entrancing silver white beaches could be reached only be sea. And each time it seemed, when the suggestion of diving was made Jenni found herself partnered by Perikles. It happened so frequently that it began to seem natural, with Sofia goodhumouredly agreeing to keep an eye on Dina as well as on Panos.

Helen remained something of a mystery, and it was hard to decide why she and Michaelis had been invited on the voyage. She was a pleasant enough girl, always willing to join in when specifically invited but volunteering very little. Michaelis too had a negative personality, but then, Jenni excused him when she thought about it, almost any man would be that when compared with their host.

Perikles, when they went diving together down to that silent beautiful world, would guide her with a firm possessive hand, pulling her along the sea bed like some impetuous merman hurrying off with a stolen mermaid to his secret grotto. With a tiny frisson of satisfaction Jenni remembered the story he had told, of his forebear who had taken a Manchurian princess by force. Then she shook her head in protest at her own imagination. How could she compare herself with that! There was nothing foreign and romantic about her, nothing that would incline him to take her by force.

Almost as if he were able to read her mind he stopped then, catching her to him in an embrace, smiling at her through the glass of his mask, putting his face to hers, trying to rub noses in an Eskimo kiss. Jenni smiled in response, causing an ecstasy of bubbles to escape from her apparatus, then released herself from his grip and darted away from him in a fluid teasing twist.

It was rather disappointing that he made no move to catch her, but they broke surface together beside the boat and she pulled the mask from her face to find him grinning at her.

'What's so funny?' she asked.

'You are.' With one powerful sweep of his arm he reached for the net that hung from the side of the yacht, holding it still so that she could gain a foothold. He watched with a sardonic expression while she climbed up to the deck.

'Me?' She gazed down at him from her superior position.

'Yes.' Holding both sets of diving equipment, he climbed up to join her, handing over the masks as he drew level. 'Yes,' he repeated as he swung himself up to join her. 'You're scared when I touch you. Even with all those gallons of antiseptic water about you run like a rabbit who's seen the gun. You're man-scared, Miss Cotterell. What on earth did Jeremy ever do to you to make you like that?'

'Jeremy did nothing.' There was a trace of the old anger in her voice. 'Absolutely nothing!'

'Didn't he?' The smile still hovered aggravatingly about the wide mouth. 'Thank you for telling me. I've sometimes wondered about you and Jeremy.'

'Have you?' She almost spat the words at him. 'You cad!'

For a moment he stared at her before exploding into laughter which brought Sofia round from the far side of the ship where she had been sitting under an awning. She looked uncomprehendingly from one to the other, from the intensely disapproving expression which Jenni was struggling to maintain to the look of sheer amusement on Peri's face.

'What is it?' Then when no one answered her tone became more insistent. 'Tell me!'

'It is nothing, really, Sofia *agape mou.*' As he spoke Perikles got to his feet to stand towering over Jenni, who still sprawled sulkily on the side of the boat. 'Just that Jenni has called me a cad.'

'A cad?' From the way she spoke Sofia might never have heard the word before.

'A cad.' He stretched an indulgent hand down to help her to her feet. 'And I thought that the word was a figment of P. G. Wodehouse's imagination!'

'Now you know differently.' Ignoring his hand, Jenni stood up, trying to conceal her own inclination to laugh. She couldn't ever remember having used the word before and could hardly believe that she had now. 'Maybe it's because you remind me of one of his characters.' And before she could be questioned about which one she turned and made her way across the deck, her cheeks flaming as she heard Perikles speaking to Sofia in their own language followed by the girl's uncertain laughter.

But when she reached the privacy of her own cabin she remembered something else with which to flail her emotions. Peri had used the very words to Sofia which he had spoken to Jenni the other night on the beach, the words which had taken her breath away with their perfect simplicity. *Agape mou*—beloved. And she had been foolish enough to think they had meant something special when spoken to her! Any more than when he had used them to the wife of his best friend.

That evening they went ashore to eat, to one of the smallest islands in the group, one that the package tourists hadn't yet reached but where a few of the more discriminating Athenians had villas. George and Maro joined them at the small quayside taverna where tables spilled across the pavement, and three were pulled together to make one large enough.

For a while Jenni sat savouring the atmosphere, not caring that the others spoke in a mish-mash of languages she didn't fully understand, simply enjoying the picture postcard scene with one or two boats in the harbour rising and falling on the water and a disc of moon in the darkness of the sky sending shards of light from each ripple on the surface.

Besides, she was confident that she was looking her best, for the mixture of sun and sea air had ripened the colour of her skin, emphasising the deep blue of her eyes and the whiteness of her smile. And the dress she was wearing was calculated to catch the eye, and she begrudged not an instant of the time she had spent in the afternoon hacking an old dress to pieces so she could copy a couture model from a French magazine she had found lying about. True, the original had been made of silk while hers was merely Indian cotton, but the result was surprisingly effective. So long as no one got close enough to examine the stitches, which did leave a lot to be desired, she was sure it would pass.

The style was simple enough, at least according to her adaptation. It was just a wide piece of material gathered into a piece of elastic six inches from one edge. The elastic keeping the dress in position under the arms while the short length doubled over to make an attractive frill over the bust. The streaky faded pink which previously she had thought dull and washed out seemed to have taken on a subtlety with the redesigning, and Jenni could scarcely avoid the conclusion that her new dress was pretty stunning.

Copying the magazine photograph still further, she had found in the bottom of her case a heavy gilt necklace and matching earrings, had piled up her hair casually on the top of her head in imitation of the nineteen-year-old model. Now, so long as she remembered the dress had its limitations, so long as she remembered that any sudden movement might dislodge its precarious resistance to gravity, then she would be sure to enjoy herself. In fact the spice of danger had the effect of making her pulses race, just a little more.

But she didn't regret it, not for an instant. For she had seen the look on Perikles' face when she had first emerged from her cabin to join the group waiting on the deck before coming ashore. Even Michaelis had been shaken out of his usual formality to utter a restrained wolf-call which he had at once regretted. And Paul had made some half-jocular remark while his eyes had lingered about the daring bareness of her throat and shoulders. Only Perikles had said nothing—but then he had no need; that first glance had said it all.

'What are you going to have, Jenni?' He was sitting opposite her at the enlarged table and looked up suddenly from the menu which he had been studying. She blushed at being found in such flagrant contemplation of him.

'I . . . I don't mind.'

'Shall I choose for you?' The subdued chatter about them faded and his words seemed to have an importance she couldn't understand. 'The menu is comparatively short—fish, lamb, chicken.'

She shook her head, saw his eyes move as some long carefully dislodged strands of hair stirred. 'I don't mind,' she repeated as her heart beat in a tumult of excitement. From inside the café came the pulsating rhythms of the bozouki, haunting and sad, an echo of the blood throbbing in her veins.

She longed for him to look away from her, for the time to come when she was free from the compulsion of his eyes. Yet perversely when the moment arrived, when he returned his attention to the list in his hands, Jenni was disappointed. More than that, she was deprived.

The food was slow in coming, but while they waited they drank wine. In spite of her protests Jenni found that her glass kept being refilled when it mysteriously emptied itself and the laughter about the table grew louder. Not that theirs was the only one where inhibitions were being relaxed, for all around them the buzz of conversation was loud, the noise of laughter infectious.

First Jenni found that she was to eat salad, a combination of those large tomatoes which look so ugly and taste so delicious, with sliced sweet peppers, oiled and herbed and with a large portion of feta cheese crumbled over it.

'You like it?' Across the table, his dark mysterious eyes seemed to be asking so much more than the mundane question.

'Mmm.' With her fork she chased the last tiny piece of cheese round her plate while she mopped up the rest of the oil with a hunk of bread. 'Yes. But then I find that out in the open food tastes so much better. Like on the yacht . . .' She smiled as she leaned her elbows on the table. 'Everything that Maro cooks tastes wonderful.'

'You have told her?' His eyes thickly lashed flicked along the row opposite him to where Maro was deep in conversation with Paul. Then without waiting for an answer he spoke in rapid Greek, presumably relaying Jenni's remarks to the girl who usually cooked for them.

Maro leaned forward with a smile of pleasure so she could thank Jenni in English, which she did haltingly. Then Dina who was sitting next to Jenni slipped one hand into hers and leaned against her for comfort. Instinctively the girl put her arm about her and smiled down into the upturned face. The child really was much more tolerable than she had been earlier, and Jenni was of the opinion that this was the result of tolerant firm handling combined with the understanding that something was expected of *her*. Even on the yacht they put aside an hour each afternoon for some lessons, and since Panos had joined them there was still more of a spur on Dina to do well.

'What is it, darling?' As she spoke she knew that Perikles was watching them both, the throbbing of her heart would have told her even if she had been unable to see from the corner of her eye.

'Do you like octopus, Auntie Jen?'

'Octopus?' Jenni blinked and had a feeling that she had hit the ground with a thump after a rapid descent in a lift. 'What do you mean?'

'I thought you didn't like octopus.' The dark eyes glanced sideways with a hint of grown-up slyness. 'You said so one day when we saw the fishermen in the harbour, when the octopuses were all hanging up on a line. You shivered and I laughed at you, remember?'

'I remember.' For a moment Jenni was perplexed, then she looked round the suddenly quiet table, realising that she was the centre of attention, the beginnings of a suspicion stirred within her. She turned with a shade of indignation to Perikles, who was watching her with a half-smile on his lips.

'Do you mean . . .?' Although she was speaking to Dina she was looking at her uncle.

'Yes.' There was triumph in the child's voice now. 'Uncle Peri has ordered octopus for you. And you said it would taste like old string vests!'

In the sudden explosion of laughter Jenni felt her face grow hot before she joined in ruefully. 'I did say that,' she admitted. 'Old string vests or rubber bands. But if that's what I'm to eat then I must just accept it.' She shrugged. 'If I can't eat it,' she looked down at Dina, 'if I *really* can't, then I'll just have to slip some of the pieces to you. You'll help me out, won't you?'

'Yes, I'll help you out.' Flattered by the responsibility, Dina smiled back. 'But maybe you'll like it, Aunti Jen. And in any case I don't think Uncle Peri will be cross with you if you truly, truly can't eat it.'

Her eyes were bright with mischief.

'I hope not, because I never have been keen on boiled vests *or* rubber bands.'

'Don't worry.' It was Michaelis who spoke, continuing the lighthearted theme. 'They only taste of vests if they aren't properly beaten against the rocks.'

'Oh!' Jenni shuddered and glanced provocatively at the figure opposite her. 'There's a lot to be said for vegetarianism.'

'And then,' continued Helen, who for once showed some animation, 'they must be hung out on the clothes line.' She paused and giggled. 'Just like string vests.'

But before the conversation could develop further the waiter, a small man as broad as he was tall, came hurrying from the brightly lit interior of the café with a heavily laden tray. He rested one edge of it on the side of the table with an air of triumph, mopped his damp brow with one corner of the red and white towel which was draped over his shoulder and began to reel off a list of dishes which were claimed in order.

Jenni found that she and Perikles were sharing the octopus while the others round the table were about to begin on more conventional meals. He spooned some of the mixture from the serving dish on to her deep plate and then helped himself before offering the basket of dark peasant bread.

'Didn't you think perhaps I would have been safer with,' she glanced along the table, 'something like what the others are having?'

'Safe? Who wants to be safe? I thought you should taste something really Greek. Fish and chips and Wiener Schnitzel you can have anywhere . . . Anyway, I have complete confidence in you, Miss Cotterell. I'm sure you'll like it.'

She sniffed the aroma, which no one could deny was

very appetising, and picked up her spoon. 'Maybe you're right.' She was reluctant to give way to him, but it was impossible to hide her reaction when she tasted the first mouthful.

'I knew you would like it.' Only then did he turn his attention to his own plate. 'It's cooked with wine and herbs, then lots of different ingredients are added— oil and butter, onions and tomatoes.'

By this time Jenni was ready to concede graciously. 'It's delicious.' She spoke softly so that only he could hear. 'Thank you for thinking of it.'

He looked up with a smile, the long dark fingers pushing a crust of bread round his plate. 'I'm glad. There was a problem, you see . . .'

'A problem?' She sat back in her seat and wiped her mouth with the napkin.

'Yes, they'll only make it if two people order and no one else in the party would oblige. I was determined to have it. So you see, Miss Cotterell,' his strong white teeth bit through the bread, 'I was simply making use of you.'

Jenni lay back in her seat and laughed, quite unable to summon up the energy to protest or to argue with him. It was too perfect a night, and besides, she no longer felt the compulsion to do so. She was just going to enjoy being in his company for the few days that remained to her. When they returned to Piraeus she must do something about telephoning Angela and. . . .

As if he had been able to read her thoughts Perikles leaned forward in his seat, holding the glass of red wine in one hand while he looked at her over the rim. 'I was speaking to Giannis this morning.'

Jenni drew in her breath and reached out a protective hand towards Dina, but the child had slipped down unobserved to go and speak to Panos at the other side of the table. 'Were you?' The words were a sigh and she gazed at him, willing him to tell her what he had learned.

'Yes.' Jenni thought that he too sighed, but it was such a faint sound that she could have been mistaken. 'Yes, when we went ashore at Myros.' She remembered that while they had put in to the small island to buy supplies from the market he had disappeared for half an hour. 'I managed to get a call to Mexico. He and Angela are to be back in a few days. Apparently,' the curious slanted eyes flicked along the table to check that Dina was still with Panos, 'apparently,' he continued when he had reassured himself, 'your sister is wearying for a sight of her child.'

Hurt by the sarcasm in his voice as well as his reminder of whose sister was the cause of so much trouble, Jenni could only stare back at him without speaking. Her eyes widened in an attempt to control the pain she was feeling and she searched his face for some sign that she had misunderstood. But before there was time to come to any conclusion Sofia called along the table, in a voice that betrayed only slightly the fact that she had drunk more wine than usual.

'Peri, I've just remembered, there's a most beautiful bay along the coast. . . . Paul and I used to swim there before we were married, don't you remember, darling?' Affectionately she put a hand on her husband's arm. 'Why don't we all go for a midnight swim? It's so safe that even the children could come.'

Then for the benefit of George and Maro who didn't speak much English she began to explain her plan in rapid, voluble Greek. Jenni, still smarting from what had gone before, looked only at Perikles, who raised an enquiring eyebrow in her direction. 'What do you think, Jenni? Does the idea appeal to you?'

'Yes.' She was still too hurt to understand properly what she was agreeing to until Dina came rushing round to throw her weight behind the argument. 'Oh, say yes, Auntie Jen! I've never swimmed at night and Panos wants to as well. Oh, please!' She danced from one foot to the other in her excitement.

'I've said yes.' Jenni tried to laugh. 'But what about the others? What about Helen?' Her eyes sought the small dark girl who was always so quiet.

'I too.' She smiled her sweet gentle smile. 'It would be the most wonderful experience, something to remember. May we?' She looked at Perikles, her eyes all liquid appeal.

'Of course, if you've all decided. When we finish our meal, we'll go back on board and sail along.' He spoke at some length to George, who seemed to offer no objection, and when they had eaten some fruit and drunk cups of very strong black coffee they began to wander back to the small harbour basin where the yacht was tied up.

Jenni stood by the rail, her hand in Dina's as they slipped quietly along the coast towards the bay. The island was a dark hump to the left while on the other side the moon hung pale, mysterious, where surely man had never trod, in the spangled velvet of the night sky.

They anchored in the deep water in the middle of the bay before going ashore in relays as the boat could carry only six at a time, Jenni travelling in the second journey with Helen, Perikles and the two children. When they reached the beach where the warm water lapped against pure white fine sand Perikles jumped out first, reaching for Dina to transport her from ship to shore in a wide arc that had her screaming with excitement before her feet touched down. By the time he had turned for Panos the boy, more independent, had scrambled over the side and was wading the few yards to the beach.

'Helen.' His voice softened as he held out a hand to the girl, murmuring something that Jenni didn't understand, but the words, obviously protective, were the reason for a shaft of pure jealousy to stab into her breast. Before she had time to consider what she was doing she had followed Panos's example, throwing her legs over the side of the boat so that she could reach the shore unaided. Whatever happened she would hate him to have the idea that she was shrinking back, delicately waiting for his help. From the corner of her eye she saw him look at her, but pretended to be so busy helping Dina out of her towelling jacket that she didn't notice.

For some time they stood in a circle, the water lapping about their ankles, tossing a quoit back and forward to each other, then the children tired of that game and began to build some sand fortifications which would inevitably be flooded before they left. Obligingly Jenni filled buckets with water, carrying them back to Panos who was in charge of the operation, and when that palled she gave Dina some swimming instructions.

'Now I'm going to have a swim myself.' She tried to pretend that Perikles wasn't standing there listening to what she was saying. 'Will you promise to be good till I come back? Don't go into the deep water, will you, darling?'

'No.' Dina was wrapped in her bathing robe now and had returned to the sandcastles. 'But don't be long, Jenni. I want to go to bed soon.' To emphasise her point she yawned loudly so that Jenni laughed.

'I won't be long.' She looked round towards where Maro was standing watching all the others playing about and swimming, made a few signs to say that she was joining them and would Maro keep an eye on the children and then waded out into the deep water.

On the way she passed Helen, who was lying on her back, flapping idly while she gazed up at the moon. 'Isn't it a lovely night, Helen?' She always found it difficult to speak to the young woman, but never gave up trying.

'It's perfect.' Helen smiled in that faint slightly withdrawn way she had. 'I shall remember it always.' And she sighed with a hint of resignation. As if, thought Jenni as she swam away from her, she were on the brink of some fateful decision, something that would alter her life completely, something that she would accept, without exactly welcoming.

And there was no doubt what that decision would be. Even though she had known its inevitability Jenni couldn't pretend that the truth didn't hurt. Ever since her first day on the yacht when Sofia had explained Helen's presence some part of her rejected it. And it wasn't entirely jealousy, although it was that too. A burning emotion which she had not believed existed tore at her constantly.

But as well, she simply could not believe that they *could* be happy together. Perikles gave no real indication of being in love and he was the last man to marry a girl because once, years ago, he had cared for her aunt. Again, a more potent stab of pain assaulted Jenni's body, so powerful that her steady crawl flagged and faltered. She lay on her back in the water, feeling her loosened hair drifting softly about her, her eyes fixed on the white disc hanging just above the horizon. How despicable to be jealous of a girl long dead! But the ache in her breast had nothing to do with shame.

She tried to divert her mind and remembered what

she had overheard Helen say to her brother that day. She had been refusing to marry Perikles at that time— at least that was how Dina had interpreted the words Jenni couldn't understand.

'Jenni.' His voice came to her so suddenly from the darkness that she turned over with a splash, her eyes searching for him as she trod water.

'Yes?' At last she caught sight of the dark head, the wet hair smooth as a seal's against his skull. 'Yes, I'm here.' Trying to conceal from herself as much as from him the agitation his unexpected presence had brought, she swam towards him with a smooth effortless stroke. 'I'm here.' In spite of her resolve her voice sounded breathless, but that must have been because of the way his teeth flashed in a smile, his eyes in the moonlight seeming unusually soft and tender.

'The others are beginning to go back.' Even his voice was tender. 'I came to tell you.'

As one, they turned towards the shore, and for the first time Jenni realised how far she had come. Outlined against the background of the island she could see the elegant rakish lines of the yacht, bobbing very slightly on the water. And drawing close to its side, low in the water with its heavy load, was the dinghy.

'George will come back for us.' Perikles turned towards her, treading water for a moment.

'We could have swum direct to the yacht.'

'I told him to come back. I thought it might be too far for you.' There was another unexpected smile and Jenni felt her heart flip over. 'I'd forgotten that you swam for Hertfordshire. Or was it Berkshire?'

They were wading out on to the beach when his voice calling her name with urgency had her turning towards him.

'Look, Jenni. Look!' A dark arm dripping wet was

pointing up to the sky and, when her response was slower than he could bear he caught her by the shoulders, turning her forcibly. A hand moved to her chin so that she was looking in the right direction.

'Look, Jenni.' His face was very close to hers, his mouth almost touching her cheek. 'A falling star.'

And then she saw it, just for a moment before it trailed away in a blaze of incandescence beyond the horizon. And as it disappeared she reached up a hand as if to catch it. She laughed, a breathless sound as she turned towards him, conscious only of the sudden touch of magic the falling star had cast.

For a moment only, the dark eyes glittered down at her, then the strong fingers still lingering about her shoulders pulled her possessively against him, the face, dark, shadowy from the light of the moon, came closer.

'*Agape mou.*' The words were murmured against her cheek before his mouth came to hers. '*Agape mou.*'

In an instant all the coolness of her body after the swim was dispelled in the torment of emotion that raced through her. She relaxed against him, her fingers spreading out across his chest where she could feel the excited beating of his heart in a tumult that almost matched her own. All the longings of the past weeks melted away in the fever of her response to him, in the urgent insatiable desire of her body for his.

She moaned softly as his mouth began a fierce demanding onslaught on hers, rejoicing in the faint roughness of his beard, in the way that his hands sought to mould her form ever more closely to his. At first with shyness, then with increasing assurance, she moved her hands over his warm skin, feeling its silkiness beneath her fingers.

Then abruptly it ended. He had pulled away from

her, his breathing was hurried, the brigand's eyes glittered dangerously. He muttered some words in Greek which she could not understand, which sounded like an imprecation.

And then at last she understood. The soft splash of oars came closer as they stood staring at each other. Then hand in hand they turned and walked through the shallows to meet the dinghy.

CHAPTER SEVEN

SHE would never sleep. She knew that, accepted it with something like gratitude as she lay in her narrow bunk listening to Dina's quiet breathing above her. Her eyes sought the stars still lighting the deep cobalt of the sky, reliving that dazzling, bewildering moment when she had turned her head to follow the last few seconds of that brilliant falling star.

It seemed to symbolise everything she felt for Perikles—intense, magical but essentially doomed. Even if Helen meant nothing to him the conclusion would be the same. For men like him didn't marry girls like her. The notion was so ridiculous that, forgetting the anguish, she almost smiled.

But it was quite likely that he could have something in mind other than marriage, so perhaps. . . . Allowing the thought to drift into her mind for an instant was enough to remind her of the bruising strength of his mouth on hers, the unutterable draining sweetness of that first kiss.

If only—if only she had a little more experience. To most men it would seem ridiculous that she had reached her age without gaining some en route, but that was how it was. And now it was too late to rectify. Besides, she didn't really wish that things were different. For Perikles was the only one in her life who mattered, the only one. Experience would have meant him. No one else. Would have . . .

Jenni sighed and turned over in her bed, no longer content to lie and watch the dawn come up. It could have been bliss to lie thinking of him, but there was pain as well. Too much pain. And even as the sorrow of it struck her, her eyes grew heavy and she slept.

The morning was another in the endless succession of perfect days, days which began in a shimmer of heat haze where the water and the land met, which ended when the sun streaked the skies with gold and scarlet before it dropped blazing into the sea. They rose and went on deck as usual, Dina skipping ahead with growing confidence, Jenni shyer than ever she had been, glad of the protection of her tinted glasses.

'Hi, Jen.' Sofia glanced up from her cup of café au lait and smiled. 'Sleep well?'

'Yes.' Jenni felt colour flood her cheeks as she took the seat Paul pulled out for her. 'I didn't expect to sleep,' she flicked a glance at Perikles, who was lounging against the rail, 'but I did.' Her face grew even hotter.

'Are you all right?' Sofia took off her sunglasses to make a more discerning study.

'Yes, thank you.' Jenni forced herself to retain control and reached out for the coffee pot. 'I'll be glad of this—I'm so thirsty after all that retsina last night.'

'Mmm.' Sofia yawned prettily. 'That and so much bathing. Paul says it was my suggestion.' She shuddered. 'I can't imagine that it was.'

'It *was* Auntie Sofia.' Dina removed her nose from the tall glass of milk so that she could nod her head seriously. 'You said it first.'

'Oh, did I? Then it must be true.' She smiled at the little girl. 'And I thought Uncle Paul was teasing me.'

'Where is Panos, Auntie Sofia?' Dina looked round. 'Is he still in bed?'

'No. He and Michaelis have gone fishing.' Sofia

waved her hand in the direction of the beach. 'I think we'll sail away and leave them.'

'Oh no, you won't.' Dina slipped down from her chair and ran to the other side of the yacht where she could have an uninterrupted view and a moment later they could hear her calling to Panos.

'Well,' Perikles spoke for the first time, 'I imagine that soon she'll be demanding that we take her across.' His eyes met Jenni's. 'Would you like to go?' She knew that the question was meant solely for her, so her heart leaped in pleasure when Sofia declined.

'No, thank you, Peri—I'm much too exhausted. But Paul may want to go. Paul!' She distracted her husband's attention from the magazine he was reading. 'Peri would like to know if you want to go ashore.'

'Mmm.' He didn't sound enthusiastic. 'What is everyone else doing?' Lazily he scratched his chest through his open shirt. 'Where is Helen?'

'Helen must feel much as I do.' Sofia's voice was sharper than usual. 'She obviously has a hangover and wants to lie in bed a bit longer than usual.'

'No.' Although his denial was bland it was as definite as most other things about the man. 'No,' Perikles repeated. 'Helen hardly drinks at all. That isn't the reason why she hasn't come to breakfast.' His lips had tightened just a little, then with an obvious effort he relaxed. 'I wondered if anyone would care to walk to the church. We could do it in an hour and . . .'

'The church?' Sofia looked puzzled. 'Why should anyone want to go and see the church?'

Perikles smiled and Jenni thought there was a sardonic twist to his mouth as he looked at Sofia. 'Not you perhaps, *agape mou*. But the others might care to, especially Jenni.' The dark gaze suddenly directed itself towards her. 'It might be the last opportunity she has to visit one of our tiny island churches.' His words, she felt sure, had been carefully chosen to warn her that soon she must return to England.

'Yes, Jenni.' Sofia was enthusiastic about the idea. 'Do go with Perikles. And perhaps Michaelis and Paul will go, too. I shall be happy to stay here until you return.' She paused significantly. 'But what shall I tell Helen when she comes up?' She raised her eyebrows at Perikles.

'Tell Helen?' It was impossible to decide whether his casual manner was assumed. 'Tell her we have gone to the church. What else would you tell her?' Then as if losing patience with the subject Perikles turned and disappeared below.

Sofia waited only a moment before she leaned forward to speak in hasty confidence to Jenni. 'Do you see what I mean? The moment I mention Helen's name he jumps to her defence. Whenever I hinted that she might have had too much to drink he . . .'

'Sofia!' It was the first time Jenni had heard Paul use that particular tone to his wife and it was followed by an obvious remonstration in Greek which caused Sofia to pout her lips and look sulky. Then with an angry little gesture she pushed back her chair and walked across to the other side of the yacht.

Paul's face which had been momentarily clouded with annoyance cleared when he smiled at Jenni. 'You must forgive my wife, Jenni. Much of what she says she does not mean. She is a romantic—allows her imagination to run away with her. I'm sorry now that I told her about Perikles and Helen Danielis all those years ago. She has told you the story?' He raised his dark eyebrows in her direction.

'Yes.' Jenni looked down into the swirling depths of her coffee as she stirred with apparent absorption.

'Well, that was complete tragedy. She was so young, so beautiful. They loved so much, but . . .' He broke off as Perikles came back on to the deck. He was wearing a long-sleeved white shirt with fawn slacks and a tie dangled from one hand. If he had been out of patience earlier, that mood had completely vanished, for he smiled down at Jenni.

'I forgot to ask if you wanted to go to the church, Jenni. I simply assumed that you would fall in with my wishes. If you don't want to go, you have only to say . . .'

'Of course I would love to.' She drank the remains of her coffee and put down the cup. 'I'll go and get ready.'

'Wear some comfortable shoes. The path will be rough.'

But in the end Jenni wore her high cork sandals which in any case she found as comfortable as most of her flatties. The thick soles at least gave some protection from the sharp stones which seemed to form the basis of most of the unmade roads in Greece. But in case of real foot trouble she slipped a pair of flip-flops into the bag she was taking with her, a capacious cream plastic one into which she also thrust a long-sleeved bolero in case the sun became unbearable.

It seemed inevitable that she should wear the cream dress again, but it was so comfortable, she told herself insincerely. Her hair she swept back from her forehead behind a wide band and now that her skin positively glowed with health there was no need for make-up apart from the merest smear of lip-gloss.

The beating of her heart as she ran up to the deck became a positive crescendo when Perikles came forward from the rail to meet her.

'Ready?' His eyes were impossible to read.

'Yes.'

'They're waiting for us.' Even the implication that despite Sofia's refusal they were in fact going as a party was not enough to douse the heady wine of his approval, so the realisation when they reached the shore that all the others had declined the invitation was sheer intoxication.

There was a moment when it seemed possible that Michaelis might come with them, but that would have meant waiting while he returned to the yacht for some clothes and Perikles gave every indication that they didn't want to waste the time.

'It will take us at least an hour each way and we want to set sail about midday, otherwise we shan't get back to Piraeus tonight.'

'Oh . . .' Michaelis looked from one to the other as if searching for some hidden significance in the decision to make the journey to the church. '. . . I think possibly Helen would have liked to visit it with you.'

'But as she hasn't left her cabin this morning we must assume that she prefers to be on her own. You will explain to her when you see her, Michaelis.' It was a statement rather than a question, one that closed the subject completely.

At first the path from the beach was overgrown so that Peri had to brush aside bushes which might have caught on her dress, from time to time offering her a hand when the way was particularly precipitous. But before they had gone far they joined another path, one which was more frequented and in better repair. They paused for a moment to look down at the yacht, to call and wave to the group on the beach, who heard them and shouted back. Just as they were about to move on they saw a figure in pink appear on deck and Jenni knew it must be Helen. The thought brought a tiny aching pain to her chest and she walked on at once.

The path meandered upwards across a plateau where she was surprised to see fields waving with ripe wheat and barley and on towards the next peak, where Perikles told her with a faint taut smile that she could be certain of a drink and a chance to rest.

'I did tell you to wear sensible shoes.' He glanced down at her feet in the open sandals.

'These are sensible. At least,' she hesitated, 'who wants to be sensible all the time? It seems to be the story of my life.'

'Yes?' She felt his enquiring glance but kept her eyes steadfastly fixed on the path ahead. 'I wonder why that is, *agape mou*.' The endearment caused a ripple of emotion to run through her and the remembrance that he used it casually to others did nothing to damp down her feelings.

'Well, don't forget I'm a teacher, in charge of young girls who don't always act sensibly. Often I think I'm the only calming influence in their lives.'

'Calming?' His tone was reflective. 'It's not a word I would have chosen to describe you. Perhaps you have tried to force yourself into such a mould. But it doesn't fit you very well.'

'No.' Struggling to be casual, Jenni turned to look directly at him. 'Then how would you describe me?' She knew it was a question she ought not to ask, but the opportunity would never present itself again.

'I would describe you,' he put his hands on her shoulders, turning her towards him as he had done last night, 'as passionate, honest, except when you allow your heart to rule your head.' One of his hands released its hold on her shoulder and plucked the dark glasses from her face. 'Beautiful—if you would allow yourself to be.'

At that moment Jenni's only protection was laughter. 'Beautiful?' She shook her head. 'No one has ever called me that.'

'Only because you go to such lengths to hide it.' With one arm he was pulling her closer to him while the fingers holding the sunglasses tangled in her hair, imprisoning her.

His skin touched hers with that faint abrasiveness which was so seductive, nudging her chin up so that he had no difficulty in finding her lips. And as they kissed she gave herself up to the delicious melting ecstasy of the moment, to the bewildering flame that began to lick with such burning insistence through her veins.

When he had done with her mouth, his lips moved to her closed eyelids down her cheeks, dropping a trail of the most tantalising caresses till he reached her throat, the shoulders bare and silky beneath his lips. Jenni's moan was not a protest, more an acknowledgment that she was no longer in control of her own body, her own emotions. She rejoiced in the sheer pleasure of her feelings, linking her arms about his neck, easing her body to the taut strength of his.

'Jenni.' At last they drew apart and the brilliant eyes blazed down into hers with an expression that was beyond her fathoming.

'Jenni,' he said again, and it was a caress.

They walked on, out of the shade of the trees where they had kissed, into the baking heat of the morning, and her hand was held gently in his, each delicately aware of the other. The path zigzagged up the hillside the peak still hidden from them but as they drew close to the summit, the chiming of a church bell floated down towards them.

'Listen.' As she stopped, turning to face him, her

eyes blazed, her lips curved into a wondering half-smile, her head tilted to one side while she listened to the mellow clangour.

'I hear.' His voice was deep with a note of tenderness which brought an ache to her chest. Then his arm slipped about her waist, pulling her close to him so she could feel each finger burn through the thin material as they walked on, Jenni confused as to whether the throbbing of her heart was caused by the exertion of the climb or . . .

Suddenly they found themselves on the peak, and it was impossible to subdue the gasp of pleasure that rose to her lips as she looked across the grassy hollow towards the promontory and the tiny monastery church of Aghios Krispos. In the brilliant clear air the white walls dazzled, contrasting vividly with the intense blue of the dome which was topped by a gold cross. Between themselves and the church a small herd of goats browsed contentedly, while a small boy dressed in dark shorts and shirt waved an admonitory stick if they showed signs of wandering too far from the group.

'Oh!' She shook her head with the difficulty of believing the evidence of her own eyes before turning to smile her appreciation at the dark figure who was so closely studying her reactions. 'Oh, Perikles! In my whole life I've never seen anything so beautiful!'

'The church,' the softness of his voice, the curious expression in his eyes was beguiling, 'was built as a thanksgiving for the defeat of the Turks in the fifteenth century and a monastery was founded shortly afterwards. But now,' taking her hand he led her forward so they could look towards a quite large group of ruins, 'now the monastery is long since gone. Come, *agape mou*.' He led her to a wooden seat beneath some trees where they could sit and look over the tops of trees towards the sea. 'Sit and rest. You would like something to drink?'

'I would.' She smiled up at him, unwilling to see him go, even for such a reason. 'But don't be long.'

'I shan't be.' He laughed and there was a shade of triumph in his voice that made her wonder. But she watched him go away from her, walking over the springy grass with that loose athletic stride till he reached the small goatherd, where he paused and spoke. She saw the boy raise his staff and point, in the direction of the church. There was a flash of brilliant teeth while the child smiled, another murmur of voices and Perikles disappeared just as the tolling bell became silent.

It seemed a long time before he reappeared, but Jenni was wholly content just to sit there waiting. It was so peaceful, the only sounds now the tinkling of bells as the animals moved about cropping the grass and the faint rush of wind as it stirred the high calamus among the ruins beneath them.

She didn't hear Perikles till he was almost upon her, but she was relieved to see the pottery jug in one hand and a matching bowl in the other.

'Goat's milk.' He poured the rich pale liquid from the pitcher and held the foaming drink out to her. 'It is good and will refresh you.' His eyes never left her face while she raised the dish in both hands so that she could drink. Its cool sweetness tasted like nectar and she drained the bowl without pausing, holding the empty dish out when she had finished. 'More?' He smiled queryingly.

She shook her head. 'You first.' It was a sensual pleasure to see him pour the milk out, then to drink thirstily. At once he emptied what remained in the jug and offered her the bowl. Again she drank, being careful to leave some for him.

'That was good.' She wiped her mouth with the back of her hand, grinning mischievously as she did so. 'It's the first time I've tasted goat's milk.'

She watched while Perikles placed the dishes on the seat beside him, struck by the careful attention he brought to the task. There was something abstracted in his manner, as if he were trying to make his mind up on a subject of great importance. But before she had time to do more than notice, he had risen from the seat, walking over to where a hedge of lemon blossom growing wild perfumed the air with its delicate scent.

He picked a few blossoms, then came towards her, looking down at them, arranging them into a small bouquet with an air of great concentration. Then quite suddenly he looked up at her and smiled, all the dark introspection wiped at once from his face. His eyes held hers, then moved in a slow caressing way over her features so that she felt that disturbing betraying trickle down at the very base of her spine.

'Agape mou.' He put one foot on to the seat, so that he could rest one elbow on his knee, the flowers still held loosely between his fingers. The spark, ever ready to be fanned into flame, glowed as he repeated the endearment. 'Agape mou.' Now he was no longer looking at her but towards the scented waxen blossoms. 'Back there you said that no one wished to be sensible all the time.' He paused for a long tense moment. 'Did you mean those words, Jenni?'

'Yes, I meant them.' Her words sounded so calm when inside her white-hot pulses raced through her veins. Of course I meant them, she longed to shout the words joyfully at him. But until she knew what he intended saying some shreds of discretion must be retained. 'While one is being sensible the whole of one's life can slip away. Don't you agree?'

For a long time he didn't answer then he raised his face to hers. 'I agree so much. And I hope you will still think so when I tell you what I want.'

'What you want?' Foolishly she repeated the words while trying to ignore the panic she felt threatening to overwhelm her. She had the feeling that some proposition was coming, some suggestion which her head would tell her to refuse while her heart longed to accept. There was a hint of desperation in the blue eyes which searched his face so intensely, and as if in response to the appeal he saw in her face his own expression softened.

'Don't look so frightened, Jenni.' His hand reached out, the fingers trickling sensuously down her cheek, reaching under the fall of soft hair to cradle the nape of her neck. 'It is nothing to be frightened about.' The brilliant eyes blazed with the sudden power of a shaft of lightning. 'All I'm asking is that you walk with me into the church where a priest is waiting who will marry us.'

She hardly noticed that he had laid aside the small bunch of flowers and was pulling her gently to her feet. Her eyes were wide with the shock of his words, her brain was incapable of coping with them. Tinkling faintly now, in the distance she could hear the sound of goat bells while about them there was a shimmer of great heat.

Marry him. *Marry him.* The words went round in her mind till finally they began to make some sense.

'*Agape mou.*' His words, his voice were very beguiling and the hands linking about her waist were too potent to be resisted. His body was tender against hers with none of that impatient insistence he had shown last night. Now in this bright half-enchanted world where she would not have been particularly surprised to see Pan himself come piping up from behind a rock, here it was she who was most in danger from her senses. She had to try to fight.

'Marry you?' Repeating the words gave her a little time to think.

'Marry me. Now.' Carefully the dark eyes held hers, as if by some hypnotic power he could have his way.

'But . . .' Her lips trembled. 'But . . . why?'

'Why?' The broad shoulders rippled under the thin cotton. 'Because I ask you.' There was still a hint of male arrogance about him. 'Marry me now, Jenni. I promise you that you will not regret it.'

'But now?' The bewildered eyes searched his for some clue about the wild suggestion.

'Now.' He was insistent. 'The priest is waiting.'

'But why must we decide now?' Rationality was returning in spite of his persuasive hands about her. 'It's so strange, so hurried.'

'This is how I would have it.' There was a touch of implacability in him. 'Once I told you that I would be master in my own house. Whatever you think of other Greek marriages, ours would not be like these, I assure you. Perhaps that is why I say now. To test both of us.'

'I still don't understand. Why should there be such a rush?'

'Because that is how I am. When I see what I want, I have it then, at the time, not later. And now I want you, Jenni.'

She waited, with her heart hammering, to hear him say that he loved her, but she was scarcely surprised when he did not. After all, most of these people married for other reasons than love, so she ought not to expect . . . 'Why me?' she asked.

'Who can explain these things? It is simply that you are the woman I have chosen to be my wife. If you agree, then I promise you will have everything you want. Think, Jenni,' for the first time there was a hint of humour, 'a hill farm in Wales, or the kind of life that I can offer you. What is it to be, *agape mou*?' And his hands began to move skilfully about her body, his mouth brushed caressingly against hers till she was unable to resist the quivering response of her senses. 'What is it to be, my sweet, my darling?' His mouth was dropping a series of butterfly kisses against her cheek as he demanded her answer.

Her answer was to soften against him, to link her fingers in the hair which curled at the nape of his neck, pulling his head irresistibly close to her.

There was a deep brief laugh of triumph before he turned with her, sweeping her off her feet and not releasing her until they reached the arched gateway that led to the very door of the church.

CHAPTER EIGHT

As she sat opposite him at lunch on the yacht Jenni longed for a quiet space where she could be by herself, where she would have peace to consider the wild aberration that had allowed herself to be rushed into ... that ceremony, with him. Even as he glanced across at her with the friendly expression that she had become used to seeing there was nothing in his manner that could possibly betray their secret to the others. It was the very fact of his total insistence on keeping their marriage so private which caused her first misgivings as they hurried down the steep path towards the beach. But when Perikles had held her in his arms, smiling down beguilingly into her eyes all her fears had evaporated.

'I wish my own sister to be told first, *agape mou*. When we reach Piraeus we shall go to visit Merope to ask her blessing on our union. Then all our friends will be told and will be invited to a celebration. That is all that I ask. Perhaps, as I said, it is my test,' he smiled with a little gesture of self-mockery, 'to prove to myself that I have chosen my wife wisely, that she will do as I ask.' And when his mouth had come down to hers, all her doubts, all questions drifted from her mind as if wiped away by some magic formula.

But now, surrounded by the chatter of the others, she felt worry again assail her. She thrust her hands into the pockets of the short jacket she had slipped on for the church service, her fingers closing over the ring Perikles had put on to her hand such a short time before. It was one which he sometimes wore on his little finger, a plain old-fashioned gold band which he told her had been his mother's wedding ring. But in accordance with his wishes she had taken it from her hand before they left the shelter of the undergrowth and descended to the beach.

'Be brave, *agape mou*,' those had been his last words to her before they rejoined the others, 'and all will be well.'

At last the interminable meal ended and Jenni welcomed the opportunity to return to her cabin, even though with Dina in a somewhat querulous mood there didn't seem much likelihood of the peace she so urgently needed. To add to the unsatisfactory situation Sofia seemed to be bursting with some news that she could barely contain. Throughout the meal she had been making meaningful gestures when she thought none of the others was watching, which Jenni took to indicate that she would like the chance of a few private words.

So when they all rose, Jenni wasn't surprised to find that Sofia was by her side asking, demanding almost, that Jenni should come down to her cabin so that they could talk.

'What is it?' Jenni tried to control her impatience. 'Have Dina and Panos fallen out?' She sighed. 'I noticed how she scowled all through lunch.'

'Dina? No. It's much more interesting than that.' Sofia almost hissed into her ear. 'No,' she smiled at Helen who had come to stand close to them, 'I'd just like you to see some books I have with me. They're for Panos and I wonder if they are suitable for him.'

'English books?'

'Of course English books,' Sofia laughed. 'I would scarcely be asking *you* about Greek books.' Then with a slightly studied effort she turned to Helen. 'Are you going to lie down, Helen? We'll be setting off very shortly and as you're not a good sailor . . .'

For once there was an expression on Helen's face which registered real amusement and her glance at Jenni seemed to assume that they shared some secret. 'Yes, I shall lie down, Sofia.' She spoke English haltingly. 'If I am fortunate then I shall not wake till we reach Piraeus harbour.'

Together they walked along the deck where the men were already busy with all the preparations for the final part of the voyage. Perikles was giving instructions in that strange language she could not understand, and as she hesitated for a second before following Helen and Sofia down to the lower deck his picture was imprinted on her mind.

He was wearing white canvas trousers and a navy and white nautical style tee-shirt. A faint wind had sprung up, disturbing the dark curling hair as he swung on a rope, the muscles on the brown forearms stood out powerfully with the exertion. There was an instant's longing when she wanted to run across to him, to stand in front of him reminding him that he had a wife, asking him if it were true.

'Come on, Jenni!' Sofia's voice, nearly as short as Dina's, called up the companionway.

'I'm coming.' Almost guiltily Jenni started down the flight of steps, following Sofia who walked with short impatient steps towards her cabin and held the heavy door open till Jenni had entered, then closing it with a firm gesture, emphasising her desire for privacy.

'What is it, Sofia?' Jenni tried to hide her own lack of interest. 'I mustn't wait. I told Dina to come down to the cabin when she'd finished helping Maro in the galley. I don't think she'll be long.'

'No, I shan't take a moment to tell you.' Sofia gestured that Jenni should sit on a chair while she threw herself on to the bed. 'What do you think, Jenni?' Her voice was breathless with the pleasure her secret knowledge was giving, but she paused in an effort to extract every ounce of drama from the situation.

'I have no idea.' Stubbornly Jenni remained standing. At this moment she had no wish to be closeted for a prolonged tête-à-tête with Sofia and longed only to make her escape as soon as she decently could.

'Well,' Sofia had no choice but to go on with her revelations, 'do you know what I've discovered today about Helen?'

'Helen?' For some reason Jenni felt a cold hand clutch at her heart. She stared at the girl who lay on the bed, whose shoes were carelessly rubbing against the cream silk of the cover, resisting a powerful urge to ask her, in possessive tones, if she would mind removing them. 'What about Helen?'

'Michaelis told Paul, in strictest confidence of course, that Helen was going to become a nun.'

'A *nun*?' Whatever news she might have been expecting to hear it certainly wasn't this, and for a moment Jenni was scarcely able to take it in. 'You mean . . .'

'I mean that she says rather than marry Perikles she's determined to go into a convent.'

'Oh!' Jenni was aware of a wave of quite irrational anger and indignation sweep through her. How dared such a colourless, unattractive young woman as Helen be unwilling to marry Perikles? Any woman in her right mind would be, should be flattered at such a prospect. But before her indignation had time to gather force Sofia's chattering voice interrupted her thoughts.

'It's going to cause such a scandal! I know Perikles will be furious. Paul thinks . . .'

'Why do you say that?' In spite of herself there was a touch of hauteur in Jenni's manner that made Sofia glance at her in surprise before answering. Then she smiled.

'But you don't understand how these things are in Greece, Jenni. The arranged marriage is everything. Even ours, Paul's and mine, was arranged by our parents.'

'I doubt that Perikles will do what everyone else does.' In Jenni's own ears her voice was harsh. 'Besides, you and Paul must have been young. Perikles is old enough to find a wife for himself.'

'Well, that is what he intended doing. Of course *he* had decided he would marry Helen. And naturally everyone has been expecting to see an alliance between the Danielis airline and the Drimakos hotel group. It would have been an irresistible combination.'

'Men in his position don't have to marry for business advantage. They suit themselves in such important affairs. Besides, I told you before I didn't think he was interested in that way.'

'But that's how we are, Jenni.' Sofia was impatient with this failure to understand. 'Oh well, if you *won't* see . . . Anyway,' she reached over to the side table, took up a nail file and began to smooth her fingernails, 'I know that Peri will be furious. No one likes to be made look a fool, Perikles Drimakos least of all, and I can't begin to imagine what he'll do now. My bet is that he'll marry someone else as quickly as possible. He did run around with Stasia Alkaios for a while— you know, the widow of Vasilis Alkaios, the racing driver. But I don't think he would turn to her unless he could find no one else. Stasia has been around, as Peri will know more than anyone,' Jenni felt a stab of sheer hatred for the unknown woman. 'Besides,' the voice went on, 'he wouldn't want anyone like *that*,' Sofia rolled her eyes in a gesture full of meaning, 'to take the Drimakos name. It would have to be someone with an unsullied reputation. She would be acceptable, more than that even, for playing around with, but not as a wife. Mmm,' she considered aloud, 'I wonder who else. Soula . . .'

But before Jenni was forced to clap her hands to her ears the door of the suite was suddenly thrown open without ceremony as Dina burst in with something of her old fierce impetuosity. 'Auntie Jen!' It was a wail that for the first time since she had known the child Jenni welcomed. 'I want to go ho-o-ome!'

'All right, all right, Dina.' With relief Jenni ushered her to the door and into the corridor with the briefest of farewells to Sofia. 'Tonight that's just where we'll be.' And a few moments later she closed the door of her cabin, leaning against it in a gesture that even the child noticed as despair.

'Auntie Jen?' For a moment the tears stopped flowing as she looked at the adult with interest. 'Are you ill?'

'No.' With a determined little shake of her head Jenni refused to admit it. 'Of course not. But I am a bit tired, so I think we should both lie down quietly and try to have a rest so that . . .'

'No!' Dina's sympathy wasn't going to extend too far. 'No, Auntie Jen. I wanted you to read me a story.' Then the real reason for her misery came tumbling out. 'Panos told me that I wasn't to play with his things again. He said I was just a stupid girl and boys didn't play with girls.'

'I shouldn't worry about him, Dina. Boys are often difficult to understand.' And with a sigh Jenni sat down in the chair, pulling the little girl on to her knee in a way that was seeking comfort as well as trying to give it. And she was possibly even glad that the opportunity to think too much was being postponed for just a bit longer.

It was evening when they slipped quietly into Piraeus harbour among all the other homegoing craft using it as a base. Standing by the rail with the wind blowing her hair back from her forehead, Jenni felt comforted by the busy tranquillity of the scene. The dark blue surface of the water stirred into ripples as the boats cut through, broke into fringes of foaming white lace, vanishing almost instantly.

The clouds which had been scudding across the sky all afternoon were less hurried now that the rays of the setting sun had caught at them, turning them gold and scarlet. The same rays cast their colours on white sails that billowed full-bellied above the decks of racing yachts.

Only when they reached the quayside, touching it with the slightest bump, did all the stir of the busy port seem to hit them. Sofia and Paul were the first to go, her sudden unexpected emotion seeming to suggest that Jenni was her best, indeed her only friend from whom she was parting for ever. Perikles, at last relinquishing his responsibility at the wheel, came forward as they were about to step on to the gangway which one of the crew members had just thrown down on to the quayside, his eyes raised in mocking dismay at Sofia's tears.

'But you'll see her again,' he protested with a secret little glance at Jenni, who returned his look impassively, 'probably even during the week.'

'But who knows?' Sofia shrugged her elegant shoulders. 'Perhaps Angela and Giannis are back by now and so Jenni will be returning to London.' She twisted a small damp handkerchief between her fingers and bit her lower lip as the tears threatened again.

'I promise you, *agape mou*, that you shall see her again soon. Jenni will not be returning to England just yet.'

'Well . . .' Sofia had no inclination to be convinced and thus deprived of the dramatic farewell, '. . . if you say so, Perikles. Then au revoir, Jenni.' She sniffed loudly, kissed Jenni and Dina for the second time, held up her cheek for Perikles' caress, then followed by Paul and Panos made her way down the gangway.

They stood watching, Jenni with Dina just in front of her clutching the rails and hoping that Panos would turn round to wave goodbye, and the tall man who seemed to be taking particular care to stand a little way apart. Then, as Paul, struggling with their cases, managed to summon a taxi they heard Helen and Michaelis come up behind them.

'Perikles.' Helen was smiling at him, murmuring words Jenni could only guess at, and to her dismay Perikles replied, softly so that it must have been impossible for Michaelis to overhear, in the same language. She turned with a deliberate move to watch them, then wished she hadn't when she saw her husband bend to kiss the girl's cheek. But it was his expression that was most wounding, tender, gentle, loving, the kind that she felt she herself would never enjoy.

She had been used. For some peculiar, perverted reason of his own Perikles had used her to get back at Helen. Or the Danielis family. Or something. She couldn't quite understand what. Abruptly she looked away from them, scarcely acknowledging when Helen turned to say goodbye.

'Goodbye.' Jenni was formal, unsmiling. 'It's been very nice meeting you.'

'Goodbye, Jenni.' There was a flicker of a smile on her face, in the dark eyes which glanced from the Englishwoman to the man beside her. 'I hope you will be happy.'

Jenni scarcely heard Michaelis's farewell, hardly even realised that she had answered, for her mind was too busy with those last words used by his sister. What a strange thing to say! I hope you will be happy. It was the kind of thing you said at a wedding . . . But then Helen's command of English was perhaps less fluent than the others who had been on the yacht. She saw them disappear into a taxi which drove off.

'Have you packed everything?' There was a formality about Perikles now that took her back to the very first days. And she remembered their compact had been to try to be friendly only for the duration of the voyage. Jenni shivered slightly as she raised her eyes to look at the tall dark stranger.

'Yes.' Misery made her voice all chill.

'I want to go ho-o-ome!' Pulling at Jenni's hand, Dina whined.

'It's all right, darling. We'll be going home shortly.'

'Haven't you told her?' The question hit her like a blow.

'Told her?' Numb desolation was in her voice.

'Told her,' he repeated harshly, impatiently. 'That tonight we shall be going back to my flat.'

Jenni shook her head. 'I didn't know.'

'Tonight, Dina,' Perikles's voice was very grown-up and stern, Jenni saw the child's lips droop mutinously, 'we are going back to my flat. Tomorrow you can go and collect some toys to have with you till your parents come home.'

'No! No-o-o!' Dina's voice rose to a scream. 'I won't, Uncle Peri! I want to go to my own house, not to your house.'

'Hush, Dina!' Jenni lifted the child up into her arms, cradling her as if to protect her from some menacing fate. 'It'll be all right, darling.' She rocked her gently, trying to ignore the not inconsiderable weight. 'I'll look after you.' The glance she shot at Perikles was far from amiable.

'Don't be ridiculous, Jenni.' His tone brooked no argument. 'We are going back to my flat and that's the end of it.' To emphasise that he had spoken his last word on the subject he strode away towards where Jenni could see George with one of the young men beginning to lash down the covers.

'Come on now, Dina.' Now that they were alone her tone towards the child was less indulgent. 'Stop crying at once!' She put her down on the deck, smoothing back the rumpled hair from her forehead while trying to pretend that the protests weren't sending needles through her head. 'Besides,' in the circumstances she had no compunction in telling a lie, 'we don't have the key. Gogo isn't there at the moment and we'll have to try to find her tomorrow. Then we'll have time to think about the matter.'

Dina's weeping ceased while she tried to consider this, and taking advantage of the brief respite Jenni seized her by the hand and began to drag her towards the companionway. 'You'd be as well to stop crying, because there's nothing we can do about it. And if you feel like sleeping on the doormat, then I don't.'

The picture this conjured up made Dina give a

watery laugh which she at once tried to disguise by another yell. 'And as well,' Jenni continued with a touch of sadism, 'Uncle Peri won't give in. We'll just have to do what he says. For tonight,' she added with a sudden quiver of fear at what that might mean.

To her relief Dina seemed to accept that further protest was useless, for she sniffed noisily and stopped crying. 'I don't like people—do you, Auntie Jen?'

'What people?' Jenni enquired cautiously.

'People like Uncle Peri. And Panos. I don't like Panos any longer.' A sob escaped while she made the heretical statement.

'No.' Jenni's sad agreement was balm for her own pain as much as Dina's. 'Perhaps we would both have been better if we'd never met them.'

'Yes.' Dina's quivering mouth betrayed a mixture of relief and bereavement. 'It would have been better if Panos had never come on Uncle Peri's boat!' And she opened her mouth in a wail of sheer misery.

The journey to Perikles' flat was mercifully short, but fraught and tense just the same. Dina was as silent as the other two, seeming to be exhausted with the emotional turmoil of the last few hours, content to sit slumped in the circle of Jenni's arm. The block of flats was close to the Zea Marina where he kept his boat and like most other things connected with the man had an air of restrained luxury.

They were deposited at the main entrance which was reached by a sort of tunnel, and at once the huge plate glass doors were opened by a doorman who greeted Perikles respectfully. A boy dressed in a uniform similar to the one worn by the man hurried forward to collect the cases which he carried to the door of one of the lifts. Jenni, trying to appear at ease, walked into the cool air-conditioned interior, allowing herself to be ushered into a lift and then whisked upwards with Perikles and the still silent Dina.

The door he opened seemed to be the only one on the landing, and Perikles' first action action when he had followed them into the large hall was to go over to the table which stood against the back wall and riffle through the pile of mail waiting on a silver tray. Then he appeared to recollect what was expected of him, for he turned to Jenni with an apologetic smile which she refused to recognise.

'Forgive me *agape mou*.' The brilliant eyes noticed her lack of response and gradually his smile faded. His sigh pained her, but still she would not soften towards him. 'I am as unused to this situation as you are.' He transferred his attention to his niece. 'Come, Dina, you will sleep in the room where your father has sometimes spent the night.'

'I can't, Uncle Peri.' As he swung her up into his arms she scowled down at him. 'I haven't got my nightie.'

'Haven't you?' Questioningly he glanced at Jenni, who explained, wishing that her face hadn't so instantly turned scarlet that their cases were still downstairs. 'Oh, is that all?' His face creased in amusement. 'But Ari will have them at the kitchen door by now. Let's see, shall we?' But before they could even take a step in the direction of the kitchen there was the muted sound of a doorbell ringing. 'And that, if I'm not much mistaken, is your nightie arriving now.'

Jenni followed them through the kitchen, trying hard not to be too impressed by the expensive blue and white tiling on the floor or the heavy sealed wood tops of the units, the rows of electrical equipment in deep cobalt blue instead of the more usual white. Vaguely she heard Perikles speak, noticed the boy whom she had seen downstairs carry two cases past her in the direction of the hall, followed by Dina, who had been deposited on the floor by her uncle while he dealt with the remaining cases. She was still standing there when they returned, and only when the door finally closed did she look up to find his eyes, enigmatic and dark, studying her closely. At once she removed her hand from the large central table whose smooth top was a pleasure to touch.

'You like it?' As he spoke he took a step towards her.

'It's beautiful.' Unconsciously she withdrew a step, moving so that the table stood between them. 'I've never seen such a glamorous kitchen!' Although she tried to inject the statement with a note of censure she was uncertain that she succeeded.

'There's quite a view.' It was a moment before Perikles spoke again, but as he did he walked over to the wide window shaded by venetian blinds which at the touch of a button were raised. In spite of herself Jenni could not resist stepping forward, catching her breath as she looked out on the kaleidoscope of colour in the harbour, the strings of lights along decks as boats sailed into and out of the basin.

'It's beautiful.' She repeated the words, then with a feeling of impatience at herself she turned away.

'You can change anything that you don't like.' For him the tone was so mild that she looked round with suspicion. Could he really believe that she was going to settle down quietly as his wife, accept what had happened back there on the island?

'Do you imagine...' The words burst impetuously from her lips, but she was silenced by a warning look towards Dina, who was sitting in one of the chairs drawn up beside the table. The child was watching them closely, her eyebrows drawn together in a frown of concentration, the thumb of her right hand very firmly fixed in her mouth.

Jenni looked at him, wishing that every bone in her body didn't weaken so betrayingly each time she did so. It would be so much easier if she could just tell him to go to hell and walk out, to know that she would never see him again. But she couldn't do that. Not yet. Not till she had told him that she understood the reason for his proposal, not till she had the opportunity of telling him what she thought of him and perhaps washing him out of her system in a wave of fury. And it was impossible to do that when there was the chance Dina would hear. It would have to wait until she had gone to bed and was safely asleep.

Almost as if the same thought had occurred to him he spoke to his niece, but without taking his eyes from Jenni's. 'I think you should get ready for bed, Dina. You must be tired, and tomorrow you will be going to see your grandmother and Magda.'

'I don't want to go to bed!' Fatigue increased the whine in her voice and Jenni fought her own irritation. 'Besides, I'm hungry. I haven't had any supper.'

'No.' At last he turned his attention from the girl he had married, to the child. 'Of course that's true. But I have an idea. Why don't I bath you and put you to bed while Jenni makes something for you to eat? Wouldn't you like to have it on a tray in bed? Then, when you're sound asleep, we'll get someone to come and sit with you while Jenni and I go out for a meal.'

'I don't want to.' Implacably she eyed him with a gaze almost as unwinking as his own.

'Come here.' Bending down to sit on his heels, he held out his arms to her, smiling. I'd like to whisper something that I don't want Jenni to hear.'

After a moment's hesitation the child slid from the chair and walked over, to be held gently against him. Jenni watching the two dark heads close together, saw his mouth move against the child's soft cheek and experienced a pang which made her turn hastily from the scene.

'That's all right, then.' The sound of his voice, firm and relaxed took her round in time to see Dina slip from her uncle's grasp, stand looking at him with that impassive grown-up expression for a long moment, still sucking her thumb fiercely. 'Now, Dina,' Perikles continued in the same casual voice, 'you saw where I told Ari to leave your aunt's case, would you like to go and show her where she's going to sleep? I have one or two telephone calls to make.' He held the door so that they could precede him into the hall, skilfully avoiding Jenni's angry look as she passed him.

But Dina seemed to have revived just a little, for she became quite lively as she danced ahead of Jenni, going through a door into a short corridor from which two rooms opened.

'This is your bedroom, Auntie Jen.' She led the way into the first, which although not overlarge was extremely attractive, the pale blond wood floor scattered with washed silk rugs in deep shades of blue and rose. It was a single bed. Jenni felt a sensation half-way between relief and anguish, so severe that she sank down on to a chair near the door, her eyes automatically noting the blue silk of the tailored bedspread and the matching curtains at the windows. Against one wall was the usual array of fitted cupboards and through a door which Dina pushed open with an air of assurance was the bathroom, tiled in cream strewn with cornflowers.

'And the bathroom has two doors.' Dina had thrown

off her inhibitions and was showing some enthusiasm for her task. 'One for you, Auntie Jen, and one for me. So you'll have to lock two doors before you go to the loo.'

'Oh?' Jenni did her best to smile. 'I'll have to remember that. So your bedroom is through that other door, is it?' She got up and followed, through the bathroom and into a room very similar to her own. 'Well, it's all very nice, I must say.' If the banal understatement meant nothing to Dina Jenni herself was struck by the stupidity of her words, but controlled a brief inclination to burst into hysterical laughter. Instead she turned to the bathroom, pulled the lever which sealed the drain of the bath and turned on both taps.

'What would you like to eat, Dina?' That too seemed a ridiculous question as she had no idea what was available in all those capacious cupboards and refrigerators in the kitchen. 'An omelette, perhaps?' she suggested hopefully.

But Dina's mood of harmony was shortlived, for she at once screwed up her nose at something that was usually one of her favourite dishes. But just at that moment she looked over Jenni's shoulder and the expression of distaste wavered.

'. . . Mmm, all right.'

Jenni turned and was not surprised to see that Perikles was leaning against the upright of the door and he walked forward. Jenni sensed a battle of wills between himself and Dina but was not surprised that the child gave way first. 'Have you come to bath me, Uncle Peri?' she asked with almost cloying sweetness.

'Yes, I have. And Jenni's going to go and make your omelette. I've rung downstairs and Ana, that's Ari's mother, is coming to sit with you while Jenni and I go out. I expect you to go to sleep and give her no trouble.' There was a hint of menace in that last statement which was not lost on Dina. 'And Jenni,' now it was her turn to be at the receiving end of his dominating manner, 'you can get ready whenever you've cooked the meal.'

But it was an hour later before Jenni had completed her preparations, for she had decided that the only thing she could wear was the white dress, the only thing she had that he liked, the dress she had worn for that absurd ceremony earlier in the day.

It was equally absurd, the hope, but wild and flaring, irrepressible, that made her rinse it out quickly in warm soapy water and push it into the tumble drier while she went and had a bath. And when she was ready in her bedroom, she couldn't ignore the realisation that her eyes were shining madly, that her hair was drifting to her shoulders in waves of russet silk, that she looked tender and expectant. And in love.

Beside the bed the telephone suddenly shrilled and she put out a hand expecting to hear some final instructions from Perikles. She heard his voice and was about to speak when she realised that he was talking in Greek, obviously on an outside line. She had begun to put down the receiver when a woman's voice, one that she knew only too well, burst impatiently into rapid emotional language, interrupted only when Perikles spoke to her soothingly, speaking her name frequently—Helen, Helen, *agape mou*.

Almost frozen to the spot, Jenni listened, hearing the girl's semi-hysterical repetition of his name, his soft tender loving responses. She had no idea how long she sat there, aghast at this conversation of which she could understand nothing but the names, the endearments, then at the very end, her own name. Just once. She had just replaced the telephone when she heard the sound of footsteps outside her door, the brief knock, the door opening when she replied. She turned to face him, knowing that their evening out was cancelled before he spoke. Her fist clenched round the ring which she had been holding before the telephone had rung, her eyes looked angrily at the tall immaculate figure in the dark suit with dazzling shirt front. Incredibly, he was wearing a red rose in his buttonhole.

'I'm sorry, *agape mou*, but I have quite unexpectedly to go out.' She tried not to see the look in his eyes, an expression that was asking for her understanding.

'That's all right.' Her words were casually offensive in her effort to hide from him that her voice trembled with disappointment.

'You will forgive me?'

'Of course.' She laughed. 'What I can't forgive,' the words were out before she could stop them, 'is that you should have married me at all.' All laughter had disappeared from her voice and her expression. 'To marry me simply because you couldn't have the daughter of the Danielis Airline—that's totally unforgiveable.' And as she spoke she tossed the ring towards him so that it tinkled across the wooden floor to his feet.

CHAPTER NINE

FOR what seemed an eternity they stared at each other, Jenni with her eyes forced wide to prevent the tears spilling down her cheeks. She saw his brows come together in a frown, anger darken his face so that her own temerity caused a ripple of something very like fear to shiver down her spine. His eyes narrowed slightly, his expression showing distaste.

'You are being foolish.' For the first time since she had known him he spoke English like a foreigner. 'And solely, I suspect, because you are overwrought, so I shall forget what you have said.' He turned away from her towards the door, pausing momentarily with his hand on the door handle. 'I suggest that you have something to eat, then go to bed.'

'Go to bed?' Angry now that her fear had evaporated, she fairly spat the words at him. 'Do you mean I should pretend today didn't happen?'

He took a step back into the room. 'You know I don't mean that.' His tone was icy. 'In any case, if that's what you're thinking of you are too late, *agape mou.*' There was little affection in the endearment. 'You and I are married, whatever you may think about it at the moment. Let me assure you,' a brief smile touched his features, 'that it will get better.'

'I can't think what came over me.' The words burst from Jenni's lips. 'I must have been mad!'

'Mad you certainly were not.' This time there was menace in his voice as well as in the further step he took towards her, a step that made her recoil. 'I made you an honourable offer. You accepted. It is as simple as that.'

'You don't have to explain it to me. I do remember exactly what happened. It's my state of mind at the time I'm beginning to question.'

'I think there was little wrong with your state of mind. In fact you were probably making the most sensible decision of your life,' he taunted, 'you weighed up the pros and cons of marrying me or Jeremy,' an edge she hated returned to his voice as he spoke that name again, 'and the idea of a hill farm in Wales was suddenly less appealing. It's quite simple really, and I do not blame you for coming to the conclusion that you did.'

Jenni stared back at him, unaware of the distraught expression on her face. That was what he thought of her! He imagined that she had accepted his proposal because of his wealth, that she had accepted as she would a tempting business deal, had sold herself to the highest bidder. In disbelief she shook her head, retreating another step from him till the pressure of the bed against the back of her legs halted her. Her lips trembled and she bit at them so fiercely the taste of blood was salty on her tongue.

'You married me to get back at the Danielises.' Again she accused him, but now with a numb despair.

'No.' His denial was brutal, like the dark eyes which glittered with a wicked menace. 'Perhaps I simply could not resist your challenge. Do you remember?'

While she gazed up at him, all her pulses leaping with the desire to wound, to hit back, she became aware of a softening in him, his hand came up to touch her, but unable to trust her own reactions she fell back on to the bed.

'Jenni.' His hand dropped to his side, the eyes became shadowy, remote. 'Jenni, can we forget about what we have said to each other? Tomorrow we shall have time to talk. Can we leave it until then, *agape mou*?'

Averting her face from his, she nodded her head, willing him to go before she broke down completely.

'Go to bed, Jenni.' She was unable to avoid the arm that reached down towards her, grasping her chin, turning her face towards him. His eyes searched hers for long intense moments before a smile curved his lips. 'Today has been too much for you—I have asked too much. But you need not have worried, Jenni.' His eyes flicked from her face to the bed on which she was lying. 'I chose this room for you so that you would be reassured. You need not be afraid that I shall expect anything from you that you are unwilling to give. This room shall be yours for as long as you choose.' His hand slipped beneath her hair, finding that susceptible spot at the nape of her neck, stroking with a delicate feathery touch, so that her carefully cultivated alienation began to slip away from her.

Hypnotised by the pleasure that began to suffuse her body, she stared up at him, scarcely daring to breathe lest her trembling should betray the strength of her feelings, fighting to subdue the urge to link her hands about his neck, the almost uncontrollable instinct to pull his mouth down to hers.

Then, quite abruptly, he had straightened up, his voice when he spoke had forgotten tenderness. 'I shall have a meal sent up, Jenni. You will be hungry, so I shall ask the doorman to bring it up when it is delivered. Also I shall tell his wife to postpone the baby-sitting until tomorrow. Then we shall go out together, you and I.'

In spite of all her inclination to throw herself round on to her pillow, to weep until she had got rid of the desperate ache in her breast Jenni felt herself nodding agreement. All she wanted now was for him to be gone, for the danger of self-betrayal to be over. But she had one last ordeal before she was to be free to give way to the torrent of emotion so long dammed up inside her. He reached down again and pulled her gently to her feet, cradling her against his chest as if she were a small child in need of comfort. And his lips brushed her cheek as he kissed her.

But the kiss was not the one she had craved a moment earlier, not the one for which her body, her very senses clamoured. It was chaste, kind perhaps, and utterly platonic. Not the kiss a bride would expect from her husband on their wedding night. A moment later the door of the bedroom closed behind him with a soft, final click.

Perikles had told her that he had no idea when he would be back, but when morning came Jenni and Dina found themselves alone in the flat. About nine o'clock a young woman appeared and went round the flat, looking into bedrooms and cleaning what was already perfectly immaculate. Jenni could not resist following her into Perikles's bedroom merely to confirm the certainty that he had not come home the previous night. Nonetheless, it was like a blow to her to find the bed unused, although cases and clothes brought back from their voyage were still scattered about the room.

She, with Dina still in a strangely chastened mood, sat in state at the large round dining table eating a breakfast of fruit, rolls and coffee while Jenni wondered how they were going to pass the day if

Perikles did not come back. It took a determined effort on her part to try to ignore the pain in her chest, to pretend that she wasn't suffering all the classic symptoms of a broken heart.

'I tell you what,' she interrupted the silence that was enveloping them both, 'why don't we go and have a picnic? We could take the bus to the park and . . .'

'All right.' Dina wasn't wildly excited by the prospect, but at least she didn't object.

'Good. Then come on, we'll go to the kitchen and wash up these things and . . .'

'We don't wash up dishes. Servants do that.'

'Don't be such a little snob! Besides, when you're grown up and married you'll want to do things like washing up for your husband.'

'Is that why you're doing it for Uncle Peri?' Dina sounded really interested.

'Wh-What on earth do you mean, Dina?' Jenni stared at the girl.

'You and Uncle Peri, being married. I think it was mean of you Auntie Jen. I would have liked to come to your wedding, to wear a long dress and to get sugared almonds wrapped up in white net and . . .'

'Shall we go and get things ready for that picnic?' Jenni had regained her equilibrium. 'We can hard boil some eggs, I think I saw some of them in the fridge.'

Just as they were going out the door the telephone rang, startling Jenni with its insistence, but she waited while the daily woman went into the alcove and picking up the receiver answered, then handed the receiver across to her.

'Hello.' It could only be Perikles calling and she

strove to keep her voice cool, unruffled in spite of the turmoil the prospect of speaking to him caused.

'Jenni.' She sensed relief but determined that today she would not soften towards him. He had hurt her too much for that. 'Jenni!' There was a shade of urgent enquiry now. 'Are you all right?'

'Perfectly, thank you.' It was like talking to a stranger.

'And you slept well?'

'Of course.' Her laugh was shallow and insincere.

'Good.' The hardening in his tone was marked. 'I'm sorry I couldn't get back, but I've had to come up here to Thessaloniki.'

'Thessaloniki?' In spite of herself the dismay sounded loud in her voice and pain enveloped her whole body. She knew well enough that that was where Helen lived with her parents.

'Yes. I'm sorry, Jenni, but I shall be home as soon as I possibly can. Today if I can make it, but . . .'

'Oh, it doesn't matter.' Carefully she concealed the hurt he had dealt her. 'There's no hurry. If only I knew . . .' She hesitated, conscious that Dina was listening to what she was saying.

'Go on, Jenni.' His voice was hard again, almost threatening.

She cupped her hand over the receiver. 'Would you run to Uncle Peri's room poppet, and see if he's left his briefcase behind the door.' She waited till the child had disappeared before removing her hand.

'If only I knew,' she spoke with the utmost reason and sweetness, 'when Angela would be home I could book my flight back to London.'

'Jenni, I absolutely forbid you to do anything until we've had that talk. But apart from that I rang to tell you that I've arranged for you to have an account at Chariclia's,' it was the name of a world-famous couturier in the centre of Athens, 'buy whatever you need, don't think of the prices.'

'There is nothing I need at the moment, thank you.' Recalling his accusation last night it gave her a great deal of satisfaction to say that. 'Anything I want can safely wait till I return home.'

'I would like you to do as I ask, *agape mou*.' The inflexible note in his voice betrayed the endearment. 'I've never met a woman yet who doesn't enjoy buying pretty things. It would give me pleasure to think of you doing so.'

For a moment Jenni almost wavered in her resolve, but hardened her heart, and of course she had a ready-made excuse. 'I must go now, Perikles.' She looked round as Dina returned from her errand. 'I've promised to take Dina for a picnic and she's waiting for me.'

'Very well.' His voice was icy. 'But remind her what I said last night, will you?'

'Of course. Goodbye.' Her tone was flip and she put down the telephone before he could say any more.

All the way into Athens as they rattled and banged their way through the busy built-up area Jenni sat abstracted, sunk into her own misery. She could hardly believe that she had been in this country for just three weeks. Her life was so totally changed that it could never possibly return to what it had been before. Even if that ceremony yesterday had not happened it would have been impossible to go back.

Idly she rubbed the spot where, in the presence of the old priest, he had slipped the ring on to her finger, the ring which she had thrown at him last night and which she had retrieved from the floor when he had gone. Now it rested safely in the top drawer of the dressing table in her bedroom. She would have to return it in a more civilised manner before she left Greece. Mentally she made a note to go in and make a booking for her flight back to London. Now that she had threatened to do so there was no sense in allowing it to slip to the back of her mind. Perikles wasn't the man to ignore that sort of thing. If she didn't do it then he would be certain to throw it at her that her threats had been idle and foolish.

They got out of the bus at the park gates and wandered through the grounds looking for a suitable place for their picnic. Jenni felt physically exhausted, but only when Dina complained about the heat did she understand the true explanation for her feeling of complete apathy. The sky, which had been its usual gorgeous blue when they had breakfast, had darkened in a peculiar way so that now it seemed more grey, and a dark oppressive grey at that.

'I hope it isn't going to rain, poppet.' With relief they found a seat that was unoccupied and sat down. 'Otherwise it will be more like an English picnic.'

'I like English picnics,' Dina said contrarily. 'Auntie Jen, when will my mummy and daddy be back?'

'Soon, I think, Dina.' It was a question she herself was anxious to have answered. 'Their holiday will soon be over.' As she spoke she busied herself unwrapping the buttered rolls which she had placed in a damp table napkin and arranged a plate with the eggs and some tomatoes. 'How would it be if we took a taxi up to visit your grandmother this afternoon? She'll be sure to know about it and she must be longing to see you.' The last was more tactful than truthful, Jenni suspected.

'All right.' There was little animation at the suggestion.

'Dina,' Jenni felt she had to satisfy her curiosity, 'you know Uncle Peri gave me that message for you?'

'Yes.' There was a momentary hesitation before the child answered, and her tone was very cagey.

'What did he want you to remember?'

'Oh, nothing. Just asked me to be especially good. And to look after you,' she added after a minute.

'Oh.' Jenni felt a wave of the most absurd pleasure wash through her body, but before she could begin to consider this she felt something warm and wet drop with a plop on to the back of her hand. The first large spot of rain was followed by several others, then abruptly stopped.

'Oh dear!' Philosophically they began to stow the plastic cups from which they had drunk their milk back into the bag together with the remains of the food. 'Of all the days to choose for a picnic!' Jenni laughed, although there wasn't a great deal of amusement in the sound. 'Perhaps,' she cast an eye towards the heavy oppressive sky, 'perhaps we ought to go and have a look round the shops for a bit. Maybe we can find a café where we can have ice-cream.'

'Oh yes! I know the one we can go to. It's where Daddy takes us for a special treat. You can have it in a huge tall glass with toffee sauce and sprinkled with nuts. That's my favourite, Auntie Jen. There are all sorts of other kinds too. You can have whatever in the world you want.'

'Good.' Jenni's tone was slightly dry. 'That should solve a lot of problems.'

They were on their way to the café, looking in the windows of shops as they wandered slowly along the busy pavements, when Jenni's eye was caught by the sight of a dress in a small exclusive-looking shop and she stood for a moment imagining herself wearing it. Then she sighed with faint regret and walked on in the direction Dina was leading until they reached the café. In the heavy oppressive heat it was bliss to sit at one of the tables on the pavement watching the rest of Athens languidly going about its business. The waiter who served them spoke a little English, but the bewildering choice of flavours for the ices was so confusing that in the end Jenni shrugged her shoulders and decided to have the same as Dina. And she had no reason to regret her choice, for when she tasted the confection, rich with a soft toffee sauce, whipped cream and chopped hazelnuts, she agreed with Dina's enthusiasm.

They were still thinking of going up to the villa to see Merope, but as it was rather early they decided to wander along towards the park and find the taxi rank they had passed earlier. Jenni wouldn't admit to herself that she wanted to look in the window of the dress shop again, but when they reached it she abandoned restraint and walked inside.

Standing there in her not very new blue jeans and checked blouse she knew she had made a mistake. Shops like this, with pale grey carpets and tiny scarlet chairs, were not for the likes of her, but before she and Dina could beat a hasty retreat a saleswoman came towards them, her dark eyebrows raised enquiringly. She seemed to have no hesitation in deciding on Jenni's nationality, for when she spoke it was in English.

'Can I help you?'

'Yes.' Jenni coloured awkwardly. 'The dress in the window,' as it was the only one she had no need to explain further, 'can you tell me how much it is? And the size.' This was an afterthought which she decided might provide a convenient excuse for taking the matter no further.

'Certainly.' The woman left them to go and open a drawer in the marble-topped table near the window and a moment later returned to tell them how much it was in drachmas. Rapid mental calculations told Jenni that it was more than she earned in a month, but before she could shake her head regretfully the woman assured her that it was her size.

'If you would care to try it, madame.'

'Thank you.' Probably when she saw it on Jenni would realise it wasn't her style at all and the affair would be settled.

'You sit here and hold the basket, Dina.' Firmly she saw the child seated and just as firmly excluded the saleswoman from the fitting room when she would have followed her inside. She had no intention of allowing this high-and-mighty being to see her standing ignominiously in bra and pants.

It took only minutes for Jenni to struggle out of the tight jeans, to toss aside the blouse and to pull the soft knitted cotton material over her head. The saleswoman had been right about one thing, she decided as she turned to her reflection—it fitted. Perfectly. The brief simple bodice with its narrow shoulders dipping to the scooped neck clung lovingly to her figure, fitted neatly about her waist and the skirt swirled softly as she walked and turned, reaching just below the knee. And the soft apple green which was what had first attracted her looked sensational with her hair colouring and even seemed to give a hint of jade to her blue eyes. It would, she decided, look even better when she wore her high cork sandals.

Without considering the matter further she pulled it over her head and put on her old clothes again. 'I'll have it.' She handed the dress to the woman, who looked only faintly surprised but mellowed as she began to fold it with layers of tissue paper, then went on to writing out the bill.

'It's such a gorgeous colour, isn't it? And will look perfect with madame's colouring.'

'Yes.' In the middle of counting out the notes, Jenni's attention was caught by the gold wrapping paper. She hesitated before turning round the parcel so that she could see it properly. 'Is this ... Chariclia's?'

'Yes, madame.' The woman completed her scribbling before going on to check her money. 'This is the boutique. The couturier side is right behind us on the square. This is our budget department.'

If that's the budget department, thought Jenni wryly as she closed the shop door behind her, I wonder what the couturier branch is like! But still, it was something of a coincidence that quite by chance she had gone into the shop that Perikles recommended. It wasn't even as if there was a name above the door—she looked back to check. Just the same pale grey paint outside with a red and grey awning to protect the clothes from the rays of the sun.

And thinking of that, the weather showed no sign of improving. In fact it was even more sultry than before, so when they came to a stop with a bus for Piraeus picking up passengers Dina's whine was almost a relief.

'I want to go home, Auntie Jen. Can't we wait and visit Grandmother another day?'

'All right.' Jenni kept the relief from her voice. 'Perhaps it would be better to ring her first in any case.' They boarded the bus, paid for the tickets and settled themselves diplomatically behind an open window.

It was too warm for conversation in the crowded vehicle so they sat apathetically, finding that even the draught from the window was humid and tiring. The glimpses of sea as they drove along the busy roads were no more reassuring; the surface was still, with a livid oily appearance which was quite menacing. One or two boats plied back and forward as usual, but even from a distance they gave the impression of being anxious to get into port as soon as possible.

When they reached the block of flats Jenni realised that she had no doorkey, but the doorman obligingly came with them in the lift so that they could be let in with his master key. He spoke a few teasing words to Dina, who replied with the faintest of smiles, but before he left them he pointed through the window to the sky, shrugged his shoulders and turned down the corners of his mouth.

Jenni's heart was hammering as she walked into the cool shaded flat. She and Dina stood for a moment in the hallway, each half waiting for a door to open and someone to come through, but there was total, absolute silence. Of course it was nonsense, Jenni told herself fiercely. She had spoken to him just hours ago and then he had been in Thessaloniki, so the chances that he had returned to Piraeus were non-existent. Still, it was disappointing to find her very sensible attitude confirmed in the stillness. Briskly she picked up the basket which she had rested on one of the damask-covered chairs by the hall table and walked with what cheerfulness she could muster to the kitchen.

'I'm dying for a cup of tea, Dina. What about you?'

'I'd rather have some milk.'

The kitchen, Jenni decided crossly, was more like an

operating theatre than a place where people cooked and washed clothes. But it was the work of a few minutes to rinse through the few things they had taken with them and then to make a pot of tea, so it was practical too, she admitted grudgingly.

'What about dinner tonight?' Jenni turned from the fridge, a carton of milk in her hand from which she filled a glass for Dina. 'It's so suffocating it's almost too hot to cook, so if you like we can go out.'

Dina appeared to be giving the matter some consideration as she raised the glass to her lips and as she replaced it on the table she wrinkled her nose. 'I think we'll stay in, Auntie Jen. Why don't we make omelettes the same as last night? And we can eat them on trays in the sitting-room watching television.'

'If that's what you want.' As she replaced the milk Jenni noticed that there were lots of eggs, tomatoes and a lettuce as well as a lavish supply of fruit. It would be less trouble making omelettes than getting ready and going down in the lift again. She reached for the teapot and began to pour some tea, but before she had the chance to drink it, the telephone extension by the kitchen door rang shrilly.

'I'll get it.' Dina pushed her chair back and dashed across to take it from its cradle. 'It's for you.' She looked quite disappointed as she held it out to Jenni, then sat, her chin cupped in her hands, glowering while Jenni went to take the call.

'Miss Cotterell?'

'Yes.' She had no idea who was on the other end, the voice with its faint American overtones meant nothing to her at all.

'I'm Chris Mytilene, Mr Drimakos's secretary.' Instantly Jenni remembered the short dark girl with heavy black-rimmed spectacles who had been so reluctant to admit her to Perikles's office that very first day. But then her heart began to thump in agitation as she waited for the woman to speak again. 'He asked me to tell you that he had been trying to reach you.'

'I told him we were going out.' Ridiculously tears started to her eyes and she turned to hide them from Dina's penetrating gaze.

'Yes. But he wanted you to know that he would be returning to Athens Airport later this evening.'

'Oh.' Jenni waited for further information, but when none came she spoke again. 'Did . . . did he say when he would be here?'

'No. That was the message, Miss Cotterell.'

'Thank you.'

'It's a pleasure. Goodbye.'

When she had put down the telephone Jenni turned round with a smile.

'Well, that's all right, then. Uncle Peri will be back some time tonight, so we shan't be able to go out anyway. It's just as well that we'd made up our minds about omelettes in front of the television.'

When they had eaten, Dina bathed and wearing her dressing gown curled up by Jenni's side on the settee happily enjoying a loud violent cowboy film. But instead of watching it her aunt had her eyes fixed on the rooftop terrace garden which was the view from the huge patio windows in the sitting-room. She had paid little attention to the superb modern decor of the room, although she had noticed with approval the group of bronzes in an alcove at one side of the fireplace, while in the matching recess on the other side was a single item, the head of a young woman. Almost certainly it was Helen, the one he had been in love with. Her head was thrown back and she was laughing as she must so often have laughed in life. But even that thought caused hardly a pain to Jenni, who was so totally concerned with her own feelings at that moment.

'Are you going to wear your new dress for Uncle Peri, Auntie Jen?' Dina stretched and yawned and Jenni noticed that the film had ended, even now the credits were rolling up on the screen.

'Are you a mind-reader or something?' Jenni gave the child a tiny squeeze. 'I was wondering the very same thing. What do you say?'

'I think you should. It's a pretty colour, but I haven't even seen it on. In the shop you didn't let me, remember?'

'No, I didn't.' Making a sudden decision, Jenni got to her feet, holding out her arms so that Dina jumped into them. 'So I'll just go and put it on now. And I think I'll have another shower. I feel so sticky.'

'Another shower, Auntie Jen!' Dina sighed. 'You'll wash yourself away if you aren't careful.'

'I'll be careful.' She swung the child round in a wide arc. 'And when I'm ready I'll come into your room and you can tell me if I've made a mistake. If I've wasted all that money I'll be so annoyed!'

But when she had showered and pulled the dress over her head Jenni had no need of any assurance that she had spent her money wisely and well. She had never had a dress that she liked so much. It made her long to go to her wardrobe, pull out all the drab ethnic dresses which she had been wearing for so long and toss them out of the window.

The apple green cotton clung lovingly to her figure and the beautifully cut skirt flared sensuously about her legs as she pirouetted in front of the glass. She merely dusted her honey-coloured skin with powder, smeared some jade shadow above her eyes and touched her mouth with an apricot lip gloss. Then she was ready and went into Dina's room for the verdict.

'Oh, Auntie Jen!' There was a half-smile on the child's lips as she looked up from the book she was reading. 'You look different.'

'Do I?' Jenni knew that was meant as a compliment and she leaned across to kiss her niece's soft cheek. 'Different good or different bad?'

'Different good.' Dina grinned as she slipped down beneath the sheet. 'Auntie Jen,' she yawned widely, 'will you bring Uncle Peri in to see me when he comes?'

'Yes. But try to sleep now. He might be some time yet.'

As she passed through her own bedroom Jenni paused to spray over her neck and shoulders the last tiny drops of perfume from a bottle she had been saving for some special occasion. Although, she admonished herself with a tiny sensuous thrill, she couldn't imagine why she was using it now.

The minutes ticked away slowly while she sat with her eyes facing the screen of the television, until after more than an hour she realised that she had no idea what she had been watching since she had sat down. She got up and switched off the set, then walking softly along the corridor she checked that Dina was sleeping soundly before returning to the sitting-room.

It was a rumbling that startled her first, deep and far-away and so fleeting that she thought that she must have imagined it. She put down the magazine she had picked up from the coffee table and got up to walk to the window. Then it came again, the deep and repeated reverberations of some underground explosion. And, very slowly at first, the building began to sway, the floor beneath her feet began to tilt at the very same moment as the ornaments began to slide from the surfaces where gravity usually holds them.

Then from the direction of the bedroom came the sound of terrified screaming. In panic-stricken bewilderment Jenni tried to run, but the floor had veered to a weird unnatural angle.

CHAPTER TEN

FOR a few crazy seconds the room seemed to whirl about Jenni and then it settled with a perceptible bump. She found herself against a door, her hands reaching instinctively for the handle, something to hold. Again the insistence of Dina's frightened crying came to her, bringing her back to the need for some appearance, however deceptive, of calm.

'I'm coming, darling. It's all right.' Cautiously she pulled the door, half expecting the wall to collapse when this support was removed, but miraculously it opened and she was able to run along the corridor, which was still tilted at a frightening angle.

'Auntie Jen! Auntie Jen!' Fortunately the lights were still working and when she pressed the switch Jenni could see the child sitting up in bed, her eyes slightly wild and with the sheet firmly clutched about her chin.

'It's all right, darling.' As she spoke Jenni heard her voice shaking, but when she sat down on the bed she felt her panic begin to ease. They sat together clinging to each other until Dina's crying eased and she looked up.

'What is it, Auntie Jen? What is it?'

'I don't know, darling. But I suspect that maybe it's been an earthquake.' Even then she could hardly believe it. 'But you don't get earthquakes in Greece, do you?'

'I don't know.' Dina started to cry again. 'I want my Uncle Peri!'

'Hush, hush!' Jenni had the very same inclination herself, but it was one she could hardly indulge. 'Someone will come for us soon. Come on, slip on your dressing gown and we'll go through to the sitting-room. I wonder if we can telephone anyone.'

But the telephone when at last they were able to try it was completely dead and the television too seemed to have stopped sending. Then the worst blow of all came when they made their way through the strewn-about furniture of the hall to the front door and found it totally immovably jammed shut.

'Well,' the need to reassure the child forced Jenni to an unnatural calm, 'we'll just have to try to think what to do.' They returned to the sitting-room and stood by the huge plate glass windows looking out over the garden towards the sea. Even from a distance it was obvious that something out of the ordinary had happened, for all the lights along the front were out, the traffic lights which operated twenty-four hours a day were no longer functioning and numbers of blue flashing lights from police cars or ambulances were dashing back and forth.

Even as they stood there, feeling curiously divorced from the panic down in the street, the ominous roaring began a third time, and before they had time to brace themselves against the shock the building began its sickening swaying motion again.

Dina was screaming, clutching at Jenni's legs as she bent to pick her up so that they could go and lie down together on the sofa. But as she did so there was the most hideous terrifying crack and the whole pane of glass shivered and cracked into a thousand splinters. Then at last Jenni indulged in the relief of screaming. She clutched Dina against her and fell on top of her as they landed on the settee, screaming into the softness of the child's body.

Almost at once she regained control of herself. She remembered what they had been taught in college about the importance of reassuring children in dangerous situations and forced herself to relax.

'Sh, Dina, sh-sh!' She tried to comfort the crying child, whose sobs slowly eased.

'I don't like earthquakes!'

Jenni managed a shaky laugh. 'That makes two of us! I don't like them one little bit.' The room had become stable again and she ventured to raise her head. The huge window was lying in a pile of lethal shards on the carpet. She shivered and tried to speak casually.

'I think we'll go through to the bedroom, Dina. If the worst comes to the worst we'll hide under the bed.'

'Oh!' Dina not unnaturally began to wail. 'I can't walk—I'm too frightened!'

'Yes, you can. And if you can't I'll carry you.'

But Dina found that she could walk, that she could run in fact when she had to, and together they made their way over the upturned chairs and tables in the direction of their bedrooms. It was when they were running through the hall that they heard the sound that made them stop and stand stock still, clinging to each other. It was a different noise, a kind of whining sound followed by a soft clang.

It was only when they heard someone at the door that their eyes shone with hope, but the sound of fists hammering against the wood reminded them that the door was jammed. Then, and as she recognised the voice, Jenni felt the tears start to her eyes again.

'Jenni! Jenni! Dina! Are you all right?'

'Peri!'

'Uncle Peri!'

Both of them screamed at the same instant, hurling

themselves at the door, Jenni leaning her face against it, Dina thumping with her small fists.

'Jenni!' She had the impression that his voice was filled with emotion. 'Jenni, *agape mou*, are you all right?'

'We're all right.' Her voice wavered but she laughed. 'Your house is a bit of a mess, but we're all right.'

'Damn the house!' His voice held a note of tenderness she had never expected to hear from him. 'It's you I care about—you and Dina. But now,' his manner changed, became more like his normal aggressive self, 'now I'm going to get you out, so stand away from the door. Both of you.'

It took him more than ten minutes to batter down the door. First he ran at it with his shoulder, causing Jenni to wince each time it shuddered just a little without giving, but then he used a pickaxe brought from the lift and the wood shivered and at last gave way.

Jenni didn't try to control the tears that were running down her cheeks as he burst through into the hall, and she made no resistance when he held her against his chest, burying his face for a moment in her dishevelled hair, murmuring words whose meaning she could only guess at.

'Come.' He bent down to take Dina in his arms and holding Jenni about the waist drew them through the door. 'God knows how the lift is still working, but it is, so let's be thankful for that. Otherwise I don't know how I would have reached you. But we must get down before there's another tremor or . . .' He pressed the button and they waited as the doors seemed to hesitate, then they closed and slowly the lift dropped to the ground floor.

The foyer had a deserted look as if all the other residents had already gone, but outside was the long chauffeur-driven car which had met her at the airport the first day, and as soon as they were all bundled inside the car shot away from the building. The streets were jammed with vehicles driving out of the area, and Jenni quickly averted her head from the illuminated pile of masonry that stood where a café had been only hours before and sighed with relief when they drew up at the dockside.

In no time at all they were sailing along with dozens of other craft out of the port, Perikles at the wheel negotiating in the dark with his usual coolness. Jenni stood on deck watching him, unable to associate the distraught emotional-looking man who had broken down the door of the flat with the man she thought she knew. The man she loved.

All the fears of the day had simply disappeared in the bliss of that moment when he had held her close to him, and with them all those other anxieties which had been such torment since that first day she had met him. She realised that Maro had just come towards her and was hovering at her elbow, so she turned with a smile.

'Would you come, Mrs Drimakos?' Hearing the name for the first time brought colour to Jenni's cheeks and she was glad of the concealing darkness and that she had her face turned from the light of the small engine compartment. 'Mr Drimakos says I take you and Miss Dina to cabins.'

'Thank you, Maro.' Jenni put out a hand to touch Dina, who was hanging on the rail, gazing back towards the port. 'Come, Dina. You must be tired, darling.' And amazingly the child put her hand in her aunt's and allowed herself to be led downstairs to the cabin she had shared before with Jenni.

While Jenni lifted her and tucked her into the top

bunk Maro hovered in the background making comforting noises and from time to time expressing horror and amazement at the scale of the ordeal they had just passed through. But when Jenni turned to go to the bathroom Maro put a hand on her arm and they went outside to the corridor to speak privately.

'You are in other cabin, madame.' She smiled knowingly and once again Jenni felt her cheeks grow warm. 'The large cabin.'

'Oh . . .' It was impossible to know what to say. '. . . Thank you, Maro.'

'I show you.'

When she had assured herself that Dina had fallen into an exhausted sleep Jenni allowed herself to be shown to the large cabin which Sofia and Paul had occupied on the voyage round the islands, but still Maro hesitated. 'You would like to eat, madame?'

'No, thank you, Maro.'

'But please, madame—a little sandwiches, some Grappa?'

'All right.' Maybe if she were to eat something it would have the effect of calming her down, because she was in a positive torment of uncertainty, expectation, excitement—she didn't know which. When the door closed she sank down on to the bed, her fingers caressing the luxurious bedcover, then with an effort she got up quickly and went to the bathroom, where she splashed cold water about her face.

There for the first time she saw that her dress, her beautiful dress which had been the source of so much pleasure, the dress which had been so wickedly expensive, was torn and drooping from the hem in several places. She twisted, dismayed at the extent of the damage, then recalling just how close she must have come to the lethal slivers of glass she shivered. Her hands shook as she reached out to the vanitory unit for a comb, running it through her hair, finding some reassurance that her face showed no sign of the ordeal she had just been through.

Almost as soon as she returned to the main room there was a brief tap at the door and she turned round to see, not Maro as she had expected but Perikles standing there, a tray with a gold foil-topped bottle and a plate of sandwiches held in one hand. For a long time they stood looking at each other before he put down the tray on a table beside the door and walked towards her.

'Jenni.' His voice held all the throbbing tenderness she had ever dreamed of and her heart gave a quick excited leap as one hand reached up to twine a tress of her hair in his fingers, pulling her gently but insistently towards him. The dark eyes blazed down into hers, dominant, possessive. '*Agape mou.*' Now the words had meaning enough to send ripples of longing down her spine. '*Agape mou.*'

Jenni felt her breathing quicken as all the significance of his words, his actions opened doors which she had thought firmly locked against her. Wide-eyed, she gazed back at him, noticing as if for the first time the high cheekbones, the long tilted shining eyes, eyes which at that very moment were sending such unmistakably tender messages.

'*Agape mou.*' At last the words which had been in her heart for so long found expression, and at the sign his arms came round her, she was imprisoned against his chest and the dark eyes flashed their triumphant adoration.

When his mouth claimed hers, then at last she knew it was real. Every dream she had ever known, all her fierce longings culminated in that tender, tender exploration while his hands moulded her form ever closer to his.

'I love you.' When for a brief moment the dizzying contact ended he spoke huskily. 'When I think how close I came to losing you!' He shook his head in despair. 'Because my pride would not allow me to say those things I longed for you to know.'

'Hush . . .' She put cool fingers to his mouth, rejoicing in the intimacy of the gesture, in the way that he caught them, holding them while his lips moved over her palm. 'Hush, my darling. It was my fault. I was unbearable.'

'But now,' he laughed, and the deep sensuous sound fanned into a fierce blaze all those emotions she had struggled so hard to control, 'I am going to insist that you go to bed. You must be exhausted with all you have been through. But first,' after kissing her again, swiftly, gently, he went back to ease the top from the champagne bottle, filling two glasses with the sparkling wine, 'first, *agape mou*, we shall drink to each other.' His expression changed as he looked down at her, his eyes searching hers with a longing intensity which she found strangely moving in so dominating a man. 'To you, Jenni.' In the end it was a simple dedication, humble almost.

'To you, Perikles.' Tears trembled on her lashes.

'To us.' All his confidence was restored as he drained the glass at one gulp, then he smiled down at her. 'It seems such a pity that we must be patient just a little longer.'

'Patient?' Her mind slightly overcome by the delicious bubbling effect of the wine, she stared at him uncomprehendingly. Surely he didn't mean . . .

'Patient. For just a little.' He put down his glass and touched her cheek gently. 'I must go on deck for a spell and I do not know when I shall be able to come down again. George will be trying to find out as much as he can about what has happened back on the mainland and while he is busy with the radio I must be in control. But I shall return to you as soon as possible. You know that, don't you, Jenni?' The caressing touch of his fingers had her nerves quivering.

Longing to shake her head, she nodded, thrusting aside the tears of disappointment which threatened.

'Now I want you to go to bed.' He smiled as he reached for the bottle and ignoring her protest refilled her glass. 'Drink this and eat some of those sandwiches, it will help you to sleep.'

'But . . .' The single word showing all her impatience burst from her lips.

'But . . . Remember, we have the rest of our lives together. Tonight we must give up for the sake of tomorrow. You understand, do you not? And now, *feliseme*.'

She did as he said, raising her face to his, offering her lips, trembling as his mouth touched hers, then when he had gone, quickly and almost before she was aware of it, she sank down on the bed, halfway to tears. Only the slop of wine on her fingers reminded her of the glass she was holding. She drained it and lay back on the bed, smiling now and closing her eyes as she rubbed her cheek on the soft silk of the cover. And a moment later she was sound asleep.

Jenni knew nothing more till she woke with the sun finding a chink in the curtains and gleaming disturbingly in her eyes. She lay for a moment, spreadeagled on the bed, bewildered, unable to remember where she was. And why. Then recollection of the previous day's events came surging back into her mind, colour stained her cheeks and she turned impulsively towards the far side of the wide bed. But it was obvious she had slept alone, and a confusing mixture of regret and relief made her laugh at herself.

Across one of the red velvet chairs she could see her green dress spread out, carefully, as if it hadn't been completely ruined by the flying glass. But ... Jenni struggled with her memory wondering if she was suffering from the after-effects of too much champagne. No, she had fallen asleep without undressing. Someone then must have come into the room and removed her dress before covering her with this light wool blanket.

Just as all these confusing, embarrassing thoughts ran through her head she heard the sound of rushing water from the bathroom and the door suddenly opened and Perikles came into the bedroom. His hair was dripping down his face, beads of water from the shower sparkled on the brown skin, running down to be absorbed by the towel he wore round his waist. At once his eyes looked towards the bed and when he saw she was awake he smiled.

'You slept well, *agape mou*!' He was assuring her, not asking a question.

'Yes.' The colour blazed in her face and she pulled the cover up to her chin, watching as he crossed the room and came to stand beside her.

He bent down to kiss her, swiftly, but she had time to taste the clean freshness of him, to long, with a hunger almost indecent for that time of the morning, for a more leisurely greeting. As if able to discern her thoughts he looked down at her with a contemplative expression, pulling a towel back and forward across his shoulders as he dried himself. Jenni tried to drag her eyes away from that dark powerful body, but found it impossible.

'I think you must get up, *pedhi*. Already I have had

to prevent Dina forcing her way into the cabin to wake you.' He smiled, making her insides quiver uncontrollably. 'She was not pleased.'

The corner of Jenni's mouth twitched. That could mean anything as far as Dina was concerned, one of those hysterical scenes which had been so common in Croydon or . . .

'She managed to control herself,' Perikles went on, 'but how long she'll be able to do that I'm not sure. I've finished in the bathroom now, so if you want to use it . . .' The smile in his eyes was a challenge she did not at that moment feel capable of taking up.

'I . . . I . . .'

'Yes, I know.' To her dismay he sat down on the edge of the bed, touching her cheek with cool lean fingers. 'You are shy. But you need not be. Here,' abruptly he stood up and turned away, 'I'll leave you this towel to protect your modesty.'

'Perikles.' The towel wrapped round her bare shoulders gave her confidence to sit up, even to swing her legs on to the floor.

'Yes?' He paused on his way to the bathroom.

'Did you come back last night?' Deliberately she turned her face away from him.

'Yes. But it was later than I meant and you were asleep. Not very comfortably, with a glass in your hand and your dress wrinkled and pulling. You had a smile on your face strangely enough. I *had* hoped,' he cast a sly look in her direction, 'that you might wake up, but in spite of everything I did, you refused. I had to content myself with a passionate kiss which sparked no response and I took myself along to one of the other cabins for a few hours' sleep.'

'Oh?' Jenni contemplated her bare toes for a moment, then she laughed. 'I'm sorry.'

Judging by the sounds issuing from the open door he was cleaning his teeth, then there was the noise of water running again before he reappeared in the door-way. 'Oh, and by the way, we're going back to the Zea Marina.'

'Oh, Perikles!' At once she was filled with contrition. 'I should have asked. You've had news from the main-land?'

'Yes. It seems the danger has passed, for the time being at least. There has been a fair amount of damage in Piraeus, but the centre of Athens is undamaged. So there seems no point in staying at sea. I'm anxious to see how Merope is. Some of the lines are out of action, but I was able to call by radio telephone to a neighbour and he says she is all right. Their area was completely unaffected.'

'Oh, I'm so glad!' Jenni sighed. 'I only hope . . .' Her voice trailed off, but Perikles seemed to know exactly what form her doubts took.

'She will be delighted, *agape mou*.' He crossed the room and took hold of her shoulders, turning her firmly towards him. 'For years she has longed for me to marry and I know she approves of you, because she has told me so. In fact,' as he hesitated a reluctant smile came to his lips, 'I'm beginning to think that she may have planned the whole thing when she suggested I invite you on the cruise.'

'So,' Jenni couldn't quite hide her pique, 'you did have to be persuaded?'

'I did.' His fingers began to push aside the towel draped about her shoulders. 'And I was grateful to her. It gave me the opportunity to do what I longed to do without having to confess the truth.' One hand slipped beneath the towel, caressing her body for a moment before coming to rest close to her throbbing heart.

'Jenni.' His voice was husky, even the darkness of his eyes seemed to deepen as his face, his mouth came closer to hers. 'Jenni, *pedhi m* . . .'

But before their lips actually touched, there was a sudden impatient thump at the door, more an angry kick than a polite tap, and Dina's voice loud with indignation demanded an answer.

'Auntie Jenni! When are you getting up?'

Perikles groaned, murmuring something under his breath which Jenni couldn't understand, then unexpectedly the corners of his mouth turned up. 'Shall I use my own special means of persuading her to behave?'

'Your own . . .?' Jenni hesitated, her eyes searching his before she remembered that first evening in his flat, when he had by exerting some particularly potent brand of encouragement ensured that Dina's behaviour deteriorated only so far. 'What on earth . . .?' she asked suspiciously.

Without replying he went to the door and threw it open to reveal a very determined small figure, her eyebrows drawn together in a frown of disapproval, her arms folded across her chest. She marched into the room, her eyes making a comment on her aunt's state of dress but seeming less assured when she looked up into her uncle's disapproving face.

'I was tired of waiting.' There was still a hint of defiance in her voice as she stared up at him, then a flicker of uneasiness as she sat down on one of the velvet chairs. 'I was fed-up, Uncle Peri.'

'Of course you were.' His voice was smooth and tolerant. 'We've all been fed-up. That's why I insisted Jenni should have a long sleep this morning—So *she* shouldn't wake tired and fed-up. You understand, don't you, Dina?'

'Yes.' It was amusing to see her simper and flutter her eyelashes, using her feminine wiles to escape from the awkward situation she knew she had created for herself.

'So you'll be a good girl and go on up to Maro for just a bit. Jenni will be along as soon as she's dressed and we'll all have breakfast together. And Dina,' as she obediently slipped off the chair and went to the door he knelt down and put his arms about her, whispering for a moment in her ear. A moment later the door had closed quietly behind her.

'What on earth did you tell her, Perikles?'

'Nothing.' There was a shrug of the broad shoulders, a gleam in the dark eyes. 'I simply let her know what would happen if she didn't do what I suggested.' He paused. 'I think we discussed this once before, Jenni. All females, irrespective of age, like to know exactly how far they can go, and I am a man who will always be master in my own house.' His lips curved into a smile. 'And I suggest, *pedhi*, that you go as quickly as possible into the bathroom and bolt the door, otherwise you may find you have to submit to a lesson on that very matter without delay!'

With suspicions that another interruption from Dina, in spite of Perikles' confidence in his way of dealing with women, was not impossible, Jenni decided that a cool shower was a very good idea, the only one which had any chance of returning her to some kind of sensibility.

When they sailed back into the harbour, back among all the homegoing craft which had been so anxious to escape the previous night, there was little sign of damage done by the earthquake. All the normal life of the great port was going on as usual so far as one could see, but an anxiety could be sensed in the way people shouted from one boat to another, giving information as well as seeking news of how the area had survived the terrible experience.

Perikles came forward to where Jenni stood in the bows, draping an arm about her shoulders, resting his chin on the top of her head as he pulled her warmly against him. 'It's as we heard, the damage is less than we feared. It was just unfortunate that we were in the area worst hit. From what I hear, the flats will have to come down.'

'Oh, Peri!' Sympathetically she laced her fingers through his, her free arm pulling Dina closer in a protective gesture that showed she had not recovered totally from the previous night's ordeal. 'All your beautiful things!' Somehow all she could think of was the bronze head by the side of the fireplace and how much it must have meant to him.

'Things don't matter.' His arm tightened. 'I have everything I want. When I saw your dress and knew how close you had come . . .'

'Oh, the dress.' She dismissed it, forgetting completely how much it had meant to her such a short time earlier. 'Now that I've mended it with sticky tape it's as good as new.'

But his words lingered in her mind as she stood by the rail beside Dina, watching while George ran along the quay with the rope which Perikles with an easy powerful throw had tossed to him. I have everything I want. The words were balm and bliss, worth any danger, any suffering to hear.

She was so immersed in her own dreamy whimsical thoughts, carried away by a whole host of fanciful ideas, that she had no eyes for the brilliant jumble of colours on the quay as the fleet of boats disgorged and embarked passengers and cargo. So that when Dina's hand was abruptly snatched from hers she looked up with an expression that was miles away from reality.

'Dina, my darling! If you only knew ... How worried we've been about you! So dreadfully worried, darling!'

Even the voice didn't immediately register and she was too startled to recognise the dazzlingly fair head, the over-dramatic style. Then her eyes moved on to the dark young man who stood just a step behind and Dina's sobbing jolted her into recognition.

'Oh, Mummy! Mummy! Daddy!'

And Jenni knew then that Giannis had brought his wife home to Athens.

CHAPTER ELEVEN

'MARRIED?' Angela's swift glance from the tall figure of Perikles to her stepsister standing so close to him revealed a great deal to Jenni. It showed pique and a hint of jealousy before it was quickly guarded, hidden behind a smile of incredulous delight. 'But I can't believe it, Jenni love!' She embraced her sister in a perfumed clasp. 'Get you!' The tiny tap on Jenni's shoulder was entirely jocular. 'Snaring the most eligible man in Greece. How did you do it?' Then belatedly she stood on tiptoe, brushing her lips against Perikles' unresponsive cheek. 'And you—how is it all the best things fall into your lap?'

'I don't know.' The smile with which he responded to Angela's kiss did not reach his eyes. 'Perhaps it's because I arrange that it should be so.' His manner relaxed slightly. 'And now I must take you to task for keeping Jenni hidden away for so long. It's a matter I shall take up with you at some length. But not now.'

Angela pouted, still not understanding that her enchanting prettiness was lost on Perikles Drimakos. 'But you and Jenni! How long have you been married?'

'A few days. And not even Merope knows, so Jenni and I are going there first of all. Then we have many things to do before we set off on our honeymoon.'

'Honeymoon?' Angela's tone of voice brought the colour to Jenni's cheeks and she would have turned away but for the firm arm at her back.

But before there could be any further development

Perikles went on smoothly, 'Yes—it's usual, I believe. And it isn't ideal with a small child in tow, so we're rather glad that you two have come back, at last.'

'You *are* mean! Doing us out of a celebration, Peri!' Wisely Angela chose not to notice Perikles' critical manner.

'But I'm not. You and Giannis are invited to a short reception at six this evening. And Dina too, of course.' He smiled at the child who was sitting on the bed in the main cabin. 'She has been very well behaved since Jenni came.'

'Yes.' Dina sprang up and rushed over to her father, who caught her, half tossing her into the air. 'Uncle Peri promised me a bracelet if I was very, very good— and I was!' She looked unctuously at her uncle, who merely grinned.

'I'm so glad, Dina. I knew you could be if you tried.' Giannis kissed her.

'You won't go away again, will you, Daddy? You and Mummy?' The corners of her mouth turned down and Jenni knew she was struggling against tears.

'Never again—I promise.' Giannis spoke with burning sincerity. 'And if we do then you shall go with us.'

'Well,' it was Perikles' voice which broke the emotional silence, 'I must go on deck and begin some arrangements for our journey. Come on, Giannis, bring Dina. We'll leave Jenni and Angela for a few minutes, they'll want to have a chat in private.' And without giving the other two a chance to protest he ushered them out of the cabin.

'Well!' As soon as the door closed Angela sank down on the bed. 'You've taken my breath away, Jenni.'

'Have I?' She turned away, pretending to look for something in one of the drawers beside the bed.

'Yes—you and Peri. I wouldn't have thought you

were his type at all.'

'No?' Jenni was cool. 'Maybe you don't know him all that well. Just as it seems I don't know much about you, Angie. How could you behave as you did to Giannis? And to Dina?'

'Oh, I knew you'd be the last person to understand!'

'I understand well enough to know that you've been thoroughly spoiled.'

'Maybe.' Angela got up and walked to the mirror, touching the pink belt of her immaculate white sheath dress with a smug little gesture. 'I've always been able to get my own way with Giannis. That was one of the problems.'

'Well, I hope you've told him so.' Jenni was quite out of patience with the girl.

'No.' Suddenly, unexpectedly, Angela giggled. 'He's changed—I found that out when I came back from staying with you in London. If he hadn't behaved so . . . so brutally I would never have gone off to South America. I just wanted to teach him a lesson.'

'Brutally?' In spite of herself Jenni could not resist the question. 'He doesn't strike me as a man who could ever be brutal.'

'Well, you don't know a great deal about him either, do you, Jenni? In fact I would have said you knew nothing about men.' Her sidelong glance was impudently curious. 'Especially men like Perikles.'

'We're talking about you, Angela. I want a promise from you that this kind of thing doesn't happen again.'

'All right, sister dear.' The endearment was not altogether friendly. 'You can have that promise. More or less because I shan't have the opportunity much longer . . .' She bit her lip, close to tears, so that Jenni longed to put a comforting arm about her as she had done so often in the past.

'Oh?' She resisted the inclination to soften even for a moment.

'Yes. I'm going to have a baby.'

'Oh, Angie!' Jenni firmly banished the ignoble doubt which came to her mind. 'That's wonderful news! Dina will be thrilled.'

'I'm sure she will,' Angie said wearily. 'That makes two of them. And you needn't worry, it is Giannis's child I'm having. That's what I meant when I said he could be brutal. I was expecting the baby even before I saw you in London. And I didn't have the chance of more than a few words with Ramon. Giannis threatened to break my neck if I as much as tried to see him alone.'

'Good for Giannis,' Jenni said unsympathetically, and was surprised to hear the other girl, with another mercurial change of mood, laugh quietly.

'You know, I believe he meant it, Jen.'

'I hope he did.'

'Are you ready?' Suddenly the door opened and Perikles came into the room. 'Come, *agape mou*, I want to take you shopping and then there are some final arrangements at the hotel for the party. We'll see you there at six o'clock Angela.' And dismissing both his niece by marriage and his stepsister-in-law without another glance he took his wife by the elbow and led her ashore.

Jenni decided afterwards that the day was the most hectic, the most exciting and quite the happiest she had ever known in her life. After their visit to Merope, who expressed her pleasure at their marriage, telling them with a laugh that she had prayed for such a happy result, they drove back into town, parking in the area reserved for the customers of Chariclia's.

'Oh, Peri!' Jenni shrank down in her seat. 'Don't you think we ought to go somewhere else?'

'Why?' He turned round in his seat to look at her in surprise. 'You chose this dress there, did you not?' He touched the low neckline of the apple green cotton, now mended and immaculate again, his fingers lingering with a sensuous touch against her warm skin. 'As I told you,' his lips curved, 'despite your rudeness when I made the suggestion.'

'How, how did you know it was from Chariclia's?'

'I saw the label inside.' He grinned, watching the swift colour in her cheeks, so that she felt obliged to show some defiance.

'I didn't know when I went there that the shop was Chariclia's. And I bought it with my own money, not on your account.'

'So,' his fingers twined in her long hair, the dark eyes bored into hers so that she felt a tiny thrill of fear, 'mutiny already! I shall have to think of some means of bringing you to heel'

'Like the means you used for Dina?' she taunted, wishing she didn't sound so breathless.

'Just like that.' His voice was low, his mouth moved against hers for a moment before taking hard possession for a long dizzying time. 'Just like that,' he insisted when they parted. Then he laughed and opened the door of the car.

'This is my wife, madame.' With the saleswoman, whom he seemed to know, he was gracious but masterful. 'Unfortunately she has lost all her clothes in last night's disturbance and as we are leaving tonight for a sea voyage, everything new is required.'

'Your wife, sir?' The woman's eyes gleamed with surprise and interest. 'My felicitations—to you both. Let me see.' She eyed Jenni with a discerning professionalism, as if she were some particularly fascinating specimen in a laboratory. 'Clothes for a cruise. Madame has such unusual colouring. Hmm.' She walked round Jenni twice before making up her mind with a dramatic snap of her fingers, leaving them with a promise to be back almost at once.

Jenni shrugged her shoulders and smiled at Perikles, who was lying back in a red velvet and gilt spindly-legged sofa, giving the impression that he was totally at home in such places. She watched him extract a thin cigar from his pocket and take it between his strong white teeth, seeing even in such an everyday action something charismatic.

'You must not allow yourself to be intimidated by such places, Jenni.' With his arm he gestured that she should join him and she sat down, willing enough to feel herself held close to him. 'Remember that the wife of Perikles Drimakos will be courted by every shop in Athens. Oh, and,' he added almost as an afterthought, 'don't worry if you can't find everything you want. We'll probably stop off in Italy and spend a few nights in Rome, so you'll be sure to have a wider choice there and find exactly what you like.'

'Oh, Perikles!' She turned round, laughing a little, and laid a hand on his cheek.

'What is it, *pedhi*?' He looked so puzzled that she knew he didn't understand, but before she could explain the saleswoman followed by two assistants returned, each of them with their arms filled with dozens of beautiful outfits.

By the time she had made her choice, struggling into and out of what seemed to be hundreds of dresses, Jenni felt exhausted and dishevelled but excited beyond belief by the stunning collection of clothes she had so suddenly acquired. There were dozens of cotton dresses, in every colour that could be imagined, some in soft candy stripes on white backgrounds, others in dramatic blues and yellows; one she especially fell in love with was a white dress in softest lawn, resembling an Edwardian petticoat with pink satin ribbon slotted along the gathered hemline above a richly embroidered scalloped frill and with a tiny camisole bodice.

And there were shoes in every colour and style, each with the high spindly heels which showed off her slim legs to perfection and which made her feel so wildly feminine. And even when she wore those she still had to look up a little into his eyes. Perikles smiled down at her as if he had enjoyed himself as much as she had.

'Now I must leave you for a bit, but there are other things you will want. Buy whatever you see. But most of all choose something special for this evening. That can go with you to the hotel and the others I shall tell madame to have sent on to the ship.'

And in the late afternoon when she got herself ready for the small wedding reception Jenni looked at herself in the long mirror, wondering if Perikles would approve her choice. The dress she had selected for what was almost her wedding was in cream silk chiffon, its flaring skirt calf-length, the high neckline of the severe bodice relieved by a frill of écru lace which matched those at the elbow-length sleeves. Nervously she turned and twisted at her own reflection, wondering if the high kid sandals in bronze were as perfect as she had thought in the shop and if she had been right to have her hair set in a cottage loaf on top of her head. But before she could decide to rush into the bathroom and unpin it there was a knock on the door.

'Perikles.' She was shy all over again. It was something to do with seeing him in that dark suit, the white shirt and red rose in his buttonhole all suggesting the bridegroom's role. 'Was everything all right at the office?'

'Perfectly.' With his hands behind him he walked slowly towards her, his eyes never leaving her face. 'You look beautiful.'

'Oh, Perikles!' Relief made her smile and she turned round in delight, feeling the silk billow softly about her legs. 'You *do* like my dress?'

'I think it is a most charming dress. Exactly what I should have chosen had I been with you. And I brought you these to go with it.' From behind his back he produced a miniature bouquet, a small shower of roses, cream merging towards pink with a few curls of slender bronze satin ribbon.

'How did you know?' Jenni put out her hand to take it from him and found her fingers imprisoned.

'I knew,' he stated simply. Then taking pity on her, he laughed. 'I rang Chariclia's and spoke to Madame Chariclia. She told me you had chosen a cream dress, so I did have some idea. But this,' suddenly he produced a small leather-bound box, 'this I chose for you myself.' The clear beautiful blue of the sapphire, the brilliance of the diamonds made her catch her breath.

'For me?'

'For you.' He slipped the ring on her finger and raised it to his lips. 'To remind you how much I love you.' For a moment longer they gazed at each other and when he spoke again his voice was husky. 'Our guests are waiting, *agape mou*. Alas! When more than anything else, I want to be alone with you.' He pulled her hand through his arm and together they walked down the curving staircase, down to greet the friends who had come to help them celebrate their wedding.

But even that ended, the day itself ended and a new

one began as they lay watching the rosy streaks of dawn colour the sky in the east. Jenni rested her cheek on his breast rejoicing in the rough kiss of hair against her skin.

'Perikles.' She wriggled, moving herself more comfortably into the crook of his arm.

'Hmm?' He was drowsily content.

'Why didn't you tell me?'

'What? That I loved you?'

'Yes.' With the tip of one sensitive finger she traced the line of his jaw, the faint rasping sound filling her with a strange inexplicable pleasure. 'Why did you say . . .?' She hesitated, unwilling to risk the spell that lay about them by remembering too clearly exactly what he *had* said.

'Why did I say that your challenge was something I couldn't resist?' Softly he laughed, brushing his mouth against her forehead. 'Because it was true. You'll never know how provoking it was to be told that as a man I meant nothing to you—less than nothing, if your scathing tone were to be believed. No man would enjoy being told that by an attractive girl, but to hear it from a woman whom you're having the greatest difficulty in getting out of your mind—well, I confess, I didn't like it a bit. That night I was forced to recognise the truth, that I was in love with you—wildly, unalterably. So I came to the only decision that seemed to offer itself. I made up my mind to have you at any price. I thought if we married, for you love would come later, as it does so often. So I made the most of the romantic setting, those midnight meetings on deck to get you into a properly impressed frame of mind. Then I thought I would take you on a spending spree across Europe, so I began that campaign by telling you to go to Chariclia's. And that reminds me . . .' Jenni found herself pushed back on to the pillows while he loomed above her, dark and shadowy. 'About that dress you paid for with your own money—I shall have to teach you to be less independent. It's a quality I found entrancing before but one that I shan't tolerate in a wife.'

'But you mustn't spoil me—buying me so many things.' Jenni linked her arms about his neck. 'I'm not used to it, you know.'

'And that is a great pity. I can't think of anything more satisfying than being able to give the woman you love whatever she wants.' His pause was long and significant. 'Instead of making her save to buy a hill farm in Wales. Tell me——' abruptly he moved away from her and lay back on the pillow, hands linked behind his head while the dark eyes continued to watch her. 'Tell me about Jeremy.'

'Jeremy?' Jenni drew in a little breath as she remembered she hadn't thought of him for days. 'There isn't a great deal to tell.'

'I did think at one time he might be a figment of your imagination.'

'Oh?' She sounded slightly offended. 'Was it so very hard to believe I had a boy-friend?'

'A fiancé, you said.' He didn't wait for a reply to that accusation but went on, 'No, not that—the reverse. I couldn't imagine anyone being in love with you and prepared to wait for some dim and distant future when you could marry. That's why I determined to rush you off your feet when you weren't looking.' He turned to face her, supporting his head on one hand so that he could still look at her. 'You have no regrets?'

'Do you have to ask?' Her voice was sleepily sensuous. 'I have no regrets.'

'I wanted to hear you say it.'

'And you.' She teased. 'You have no regrets? After

all, a marriage to Helen would have brought you bene-
fits which marrying an English schoolteacher can
hardly measure up to. People seemed convinced you
would marry Helen. Sofia could hardly hide her
amazement when she came to the reception.' Jenni
giggled. 'She was desperately trying to remember
exactly what she'd told me about you and Helen.'

'But I have told you there never was any chance of
that. I like Helen, but she is a child. Even if I had not
met you I could never have married her. Her father
had the idea that it would make sense, but the suggestion pleased neither of us. Besides, she was already in
love with one of the pilots on their airline and . . .'

'In love? But I thought she was joining a religious
order.' The story as related by Sofia was becoming
even more complicated.

'No, that was simply her last threat to make her
father give way. And that is why I had to rush off to
Thessaloniki. When she rang me she was on the verge
of hysteria, threatening to do something desperate if I
didn't go up and explain to her father that we would
never marry. Of course I shouldn't have gone, but I
was disturbed by the wall that had suddenly been
erected between us, *pedhi*.' His fingers moved over her
cheeks. 'So I went up north and explained that as I
already had a wife marriage to Helen was out of the
question.'

'A wife.' Jenni savoured the word, repeating it in
her mind once or twice for her own satisfaction. 'Do
you really mean that, Perikles? Are we truly married?'

'Of course we are.' His arm tightened about her.
'Don't tell me at this late stage that you're in the habit
of spending the night with men to whom you are not
married!'

'Only if they're you, Perikles,' she said, with more

emotion and less attention to grammar than might have been expected. 'You have no regrets?' She repeated the question she had asked earlier.

'Do *you* have to ask?' Beneath the tantalising touch of his mouth her lips tembled as she received her answer and she reached up her arms to pull his face closer to hers.

'*Sagapo*. Sagapo, *agape mou.*'

'*Sagapo*—I love you. *Sagapo.*'

THESEUS AND THE MINOTAUR

In *Catch a Star* little Dina pleads with a reluctant Jenni to tell the story of the Minotaur. In Greek mythology the Minotaur was a horrible monster with the head of a bull and the body of a man. How Theseus became a hero by slaying the Minotaur is a tale that has fascinated children for centuries.

Theseus was a strong and handsome young prince, the son of King Aegeus of Athens. The Athenians suffered a dreadful misfortune; having lost a war against King Minos of Crete, they were required to pay a tribute: each year seven youths and seven maidens were delivered to Minos. In his palace at Knossos, these unfortunate young men and women were put into the labyrinth, which was a maze of corridors that seemed to have no beginning and no end, and from which it was impossible to escape. And in the labyrinth roamed the Minotaur, who devoured the unfortunate young Athenians.

Theseus vowed to rid his father's people of this monster. When it came time to send the tribute to Crete, he offered himself as one of the youths. At Knossos, Minos's daughter, Ariadne, saw the handsome prince and fell in love with him. She gave him a sword to kill the Minotaur, as well as some thread to string behind him in the labyrinth so he could find his way out.

Theseus did kill the Minotaur, and he returned to his father's kingdom to eventually become the King of Athens. And while most of Theseus's story is a fable—certainly there has never been a real Minotaur—it is based on a real Athenian king who is remembered by history as a kind and benevolent leader.

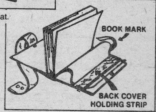